How the Butcher Bird Finds Her Voice

A Novel

How the Butcher Bird Finds Her Voice

Markus Egeler Jones

Five Oaks Press
FIVE-OAKS-PRESS.COM

ISBN: 978-1-944355-43-2

Five Oaks Press
Newburgh, NY 12550
five-oaks-press.com
editor@five-oaks-press.com

Cover Art: Bryce Belinte

Cover Design: Alex Waterworth

Author photo: Mary Clai Jones

Interior Layout: Lynn Houston

Printed in the U.S.A.

This novel is for my grandmother—
Lass Märchen kommen, Oma . . .

CONTENTS

If You Chase Two Rabbits, You Will Lose Them Both   1

For These Are Wells Without Water   17

The Men with Painted Faces   29

The Dead Indian   46

The Tale of Cindy Jack's Mother   59

Old Man Gloom   67

Trash   75

How the Butcher Bird Finds Her Voice   79

Cindy Jack and the Town Drunks   83

1952   95

Before Following Your Vengeance, Dig Two Graves   107

The Hunter   117

Transmigration   137

Before I tell you the dream stories of Chicken Noodle, Cindy Jack, and the man in the sunglasses, it is important to begin by saying stories in general have no beginning and no ending, and although the names of characters and places change the stories stay the same. Stories deal with hozho, the circle and balance of life, the depths and layers of harmony, the opposite of discord. It is an elemental rightness, a sense of belonging even in times of deep antipathy. Stories envelope the early days of Sun and Moon and days earlier even, days of other worldly origin where they are our only memory of time long past. The balance of everything is not only connected to a fluid past but a continuous future. Many stories are connected over and over and over again, and thus Chicken Noodle, like anyone, is connected to first woman, first man, and story itself.

If You Chase Two Rabbits,
You Will Lose Them Both

Their daughter sat at the kitchen table. She spoon-fed Chicken Noodle, their grandson, something mashed up and green. The toddler held on to a clean spoon, upside down and backwards. Early morning light cut through the windows of the room, soft but bright. His daughter turned in her chair and smiled at George. It was a sad smile. It was the smile you made when holding the hand of someone who, having lived a long life, lay in bed waiting for the surprise of their last breath. He wanted to lean over and kiss his daughter on the top of her head, to somehow assure her they would find their way together again.

"It's your daughter or those snakes," his wife said. "No discussion."

A skinny table with short legs sat next to the wall under the window. Many plants, mostly herbs, grew there. They reached with their tiny stems toward the sunlight. The creeping zinnia bunched and crowded itself out of its own pot. Finger nail clippings, marbles, and pebbles—all sorts of tiny bits of debris—littered the soil of the pots. Some of the sprouting herbs were fatigued and battle worn, stems broken and leaves missing. Chicken Noodle used the short table for wobbly toddler pull-ups. He crawled to the table and pulled himself up onto his feet. Once on his feet he didn't know how to let go and sometimes an herb or two grabbed onto him and he and the plants spilled to the rug. The plants spiraled to the floor so many times George wondered why his wife didn't move them someplace higher.

"Kaila, it's a woman's curse," his wife told their daughter, "to continue caring for men, even when they grow old."

His wife wrapped silver foil around a burrito at the counter. She handed him the wrap. It smelled like greased iron. Her eyes glowed, an animal's eyes reflecting headlights at night.

"No discussion," she said, "Get rid of them."

His wife was short and unsmiling. Her long and wild hair whipped around, caught in a wind of her own movement. She wasn't old yet. But like his, the lines in her face were deepening. She had never been very pretty. She was only sometimes funny. She couldn't really cook. She made burritos. That was it. They had never really talked. He married her when he was young. Before it all became a mess. They didn't know each other. She, like her mother, could tell stories. He had loved that about her. She didn't tell stories anymore.

He grabbed his hat and let the screen door bang into its frame as he walked to his green Ford Ranger. The screen door was a beaver smacking its tail on the water in warning. A ball of yarn on a slate of blue, the orange sun floated up from the mountains into the sky.

He spent days wandering creek beds to relive, step for step, his childhood. Stories, old stories, forgotten stories, nagged and tugged at his memory. He watched a bald eagle stare across the red rocky stretch of desert and he listened for a coyote yip. The yips carried across the desert less often now. Ranchers killed the coyote in lockstep with the rattlesnake. Both were feared animals, but the stories of Coyote stealing the Sun and Moon and other mischief always left George fond of old man Coyote, and, of course, he liked his snakes. *Avoid all snakes*, his own grandfather said long ago. *Always shuffle your feet.* George strained to hear the yips. He hoped to catch another story out of the desert air. As kids, he and his wife heard the same stories. They shared that connection to the past. Her mother had been a story teller. Her mother's mother had been a story teller. She wove scenes right into the air as if they were life itself.

Rain. Long gray smudges, the horizon smeared with an old chalk board eraser, moved slowly. Clouds hung. There was a buildup, a thunderhead towered, and soon it arrived.

Kaila loved the way rain moved. Before he went to war, they explored the desert together. Since he came back, she had no interest.

When she was little, she begged George to drive her, to chase those slanted streaks of rain. Sometimes a bit of luck turned a band of rain their direction. She squealed when drops splashed onto the windshield. Well, she had no interest now. For a time, right after his back healed, they rediscovered some of her childhood loves. They sat in the cab of the truck when it rained. They wouldn't go anywhere. They just sat in the yard and listened to the rain bounce off the glass and metal of the cab and watch it splash down the windshield.

"Daddy," she said, "I'm glad you're home."

Then she told him stories of change. Some stories, like the assassination, happened right before he left in '63. He listened anyway. In the span of a week, she covered his lost decade, everything from the space program to rock and roll. She and Sam were enamored with the moon landing and each other. Then there was Woodstock and through it all he listened to her. Of course he knew all these things, everything except for the boyfriend. Soldiers sacrificed much, but newspapers, at least the odd clipping from a home town paper, made the rounds during the day. She described the new Catholic school being built in town and taking a fieldtrip, sitting on the bus with Sam, to the Sandia Peak tramway which had also been built while he was away.

"Sam showed me."

"Showed you what?"

"Albuquerque. You can see it," her voice lifted with excitement, "and the whole desert, all the way to the end. You would love the desert from up there."

She retold her Kinaalda. George kept his head down as she talked. His fingers squeezed the steering wheel. She giggled as she remembered grinding corn and the old women not letting her dress herself. They painted her with clay. The cool white clay made an impression on her as it dried and baked right on her skin. George thought about walking waist deep through the muddy places of the jungle.

"They kept combing my hair," she said, "they washed it and combed it and my head felt light." She twisted the ends of her hair with her fingers. "It was like my hair floated on top of my head."

She spoke of Changing Woman, mother earth, and of ritual and dance and music. Just the shift in subjects, from new buildings in town to this ceremony, told George how great the shift from childhood to womanhood had been and how much Kaila changed and how much he missed.

"Sam says . . ." she picked at a stitch tucked into the seam of the leather seat.

"Sam this and Sam that," he said. The interruption boomed through the cab, a clap of thunder vibrating down to earth. He didn't know why. He knew where the anger came from. It was part of being the bogey man. He knew she wasn't a child anymore. What he knew most of all was that he had lost a part of his life, and it was life he could never get back.

After that Kaila stopped telling him stories in the cab of his truck, so George picked his way out of gullies on his own. His boots slid on the rock, his good arm grabbed hold of a boulder edge and pulled him up the bank, while his bad arm held his Stetson on his head. Thunder boomed. It reminded him of other booms. There was the fox. She sat off to his side on a big rock in the sun. She watched him. Her eyes didn't shine, glassy, like an animal's. Days and weeks slipped by without a trace of her and he stopped thinking about her. When the memory of her seemed to have gone underground, when her image barely reverberated from the small cave in the back of his mind, she reappeared blinking as if stepping into sunlight.

At the top of the rise, he stood to watch the rain—spots of blue sky parted the marauding rain bands. He didn't move like he did before. He didn't know how to anymore. His dusty boot prints dotted with raindrops. The drops reminded him of his last jump. The fox could always do that—project a scene from his past onto the blank screen of his mind and he always looked on, like staring through glass into his own world.

His last jump gave a lot of blood to the earth. He hung there all netted in the canopy. Blood dripped onto the big green leaves around his feet. Parachute and lines tangled all around him. His arm was pinned behind his back by a branch at the last second and smacked him into the trunk.

"Boy, you's lucky," his lieutenant said. "A mouse could a farted that arm off."

Several times during his years of recovery, he was told it was a miracle he didn't lose his arm. The first time he heard it the same doctor told another man, a couple cots down, the same thing about that man's penis.

"It's a miracle you didn't lose Jimmy down there," the doctor said. "Don't ever try and cut it off again. You only have one of those, unlike the Indian there." He nodded at George's good arm, "he's got a spare."

George remembered their tent to be more jungle than hospital.

George couldn't move because of his back. He just stared at the sagging canvas. He couldn't move for months even after being shipped home. Lying on his back, he followed seams, or cracks, or any semblance of a path with his eyes. He hunted insects. Setting up imaginary ambushes and the best places to stalk the leggy bugs was not nearly as good as being out and doing the real thing, but it passed the time. George also placed cities and camps along the creases of the canvas. By the end of his stay, all of Vietnam was mapped on the ceiling of his hospital tent.

It was always hot. He was always sticky. His arm was big. It smelled like a mud pit. It was three, four times its normal size all wrapped in bandages. A giant leech attached to his shoulder. Its great underbelly, sagging and wet, oozed a mix of fluid.

After the helicopters came in to pick him up, and after the drip wore off, and after he could think, he found out he broke his back.

Years later, when he met up with Raul Jack, he shared the stories. Raul shared his own stories. Every so often they met in town, in the morning, for coffee. Afterwards and alone in the cab of his truck, George replayed in his mind looped scenes of war during his long drive home.

Raul was very thin. He had a bent nose and small eyes. His hair stayed tied up in a ponytail most days. Shirts hung from his shoulders like from a stretched clothesline. Sometimes they only talked about the weather and the white hippies moving to town. Sometimes they talked about the jungle. They didn't know each other before they went to war. Raul was almost ten years younger than George and had come into the war at the very end, when it was the messiest. George figured it didn't matter if you were there a day or a year or a decade—it wound its way, a poisonous vine, into the secret places inside a man.

"The thing is," Raul often said, "we got to figure out how to forgive ourselves."

George told Raul about the man with the miraculous penis. He was a little man. He was a nervous man. The two convalescing men shared stories the weeks they were together. They were both to be discharged. Years of rehabilitation awaited George in stateside hospitals.

George told Raul the penis story at McDonalds. He sat there blowing the steam from his coffee sitting on the orange plastic table top.

"So?" George asked the penis man. It was the day before they shipped George home.

"Man, you don't wanna know." The man lay sideways, facing George, on his cot. He lay that way most days.

George nodded that he did want to know.

"Well, we'd been getting rowdy in town during R&R, so one of the officers had a few tents put up and brought some of the whores to stay just outside camp."

George placed the sex tents on the right side of the canvas hanging over his head. He placed his imaginary bordello to the right of the long legged ant highway, the stitched seam running along the canvas corner they used to traverse. He put it right in the middle of the wet looking stain that never dried up.

"So we had a day, you know," the little man said, "after drinking beer and playing cards and smoking joints a couple of the fellas decided to wander over to those tents."

Raul had several stories with tents similar to these as the backdrop to more shit than George wanted to stomach, more self-forgiveness than George wanted to consider.

"Anyway, one of the boys came out of a tent drunk as shit and said 'that one just lays there. It's all wham, bam, thank you ma'am.'" The man emphasized the last few words by pounding his fist into his palm. "I was drunk and tired and was just looking for pussy, so I figured that was the tent for me."

The man never smiled as he told his story.

"I crawl in there and sure enough she don't move," he said. "It creeped me out, she being so quiet."

In the end, he pulled her from the tent and yelled for a doctor.

"Doc said she died of leprosy."

The man pulled out his knife to cut off his own penis.

He explained to George, "No way I was bringing that back home to the girlfriend." He didn't get far before some soldiers nearby wrested his knife away. By then, there was a lot of blood.

When George finished the penis story, Raul laughed and wondered how that talk back home would have gone. "Hey baby," he said, "I'm back, but I left my dick in Nam."

George worried about bringing home the bogey man. To him, it was more real than leprosy. If only he could have left that in Vietnam.

The desert didn't care how broken he was.

His little girl had been a little girl with braids when he left at the beginning of it all. Now she was a woman, and the tips of her loose brown hair played around her shoulders. War was greedy. It took everything. It took away all the little bits of one's life. It took away his little girl. Not long after she quit talking to him he found out she was pregnant. Everything but broth made her sick. He even made her sick. They ate soup every day for nine months. His wife started calling the unborn baby Chicken Noodle.

Bright sunlight flooded the windows the moment Chicken Noodle was born. At first, George listened to his wife moving through the house. She talked to Kaila or the child, but he could only hear her voice through the walls, not the words. He got up and out of bed.

His wife closed Kaila's door.

He crossed the room back to his bed, and he slithered back under his covers.

Kaila hated him for his absence.

"Daddy, it's not true," she would say.

But it was true. She did hate him. Those first few years back were clouded in a clinking of glass bottles. His bottles collected on the window sill and on the floor. They marched from his room like a trail of ants to line the back of the toilet and help hold down the peeling laminate counter in the kitchen. After their fight about the boy, she tried, for a while, to hide his beer. George saw her at the bedroom door and she asked to hike out to the desert or sit in the truck again while it rained. She stood there leaning on the door sill. He lay there in bed staring at the ceiling. The bogey man hardened his heart. At some point, he didn't know when, she stopped trying. He just lay there on his back, planning ambushes on the adobe plaster ceiling of his room.

George watched the rain from under a sage brush. The roots of the silver sage spidered out of a split in the boulder above him, and the thick trunk leaned out like a sentry with a hand over its eyes to block out sun or rain. Together he and the sage watched the rain. Most of the rain evaporated before it hit the ground. The small tree was enough cover. He pulled a water bottle from his pack. Looking at the burrito his wife made that morning, he decided he wasn't hungry.

Early summer was already hot. The dens along the way were empty. He learned to track and follow most everything in the desert. He learned from his father who learned from his father who learned from his father.

He had a soft spot for the western rattlesnake. Most ranchers killed them on sight. George brought a few home every summer. After he quit drinking, he thought about the fighting too much. He felt empty. Without them something dangerous escaped from his life. It wasn't like that before the war, but it was like that now.

"It'll be the baby or the snakes," his daughter had said. She placed her hands on her belly. She was a skinny kid with a great big belly. He hadn't heard the end of it since she made that comment a couple years back. His wife picked up on his hesitation and used it against him.

"What will be?" he asked.

"Your decision."

George didn't understand that connection.

"Maybe I should move closer to town anyway," she said.

"Don't be silly," his wife replied to their daughter. She looked at George. "That old snake will go. He and his brood."

He wasn't sure if he could let the snakes go.

In some of the dark moments, in some of the wet, dark moments when he was laying there in a soggy patch, leeches sucking up to every part of his body, even his balls, he had watched women across the fields talk covering their mouths with their hands. The way they talked reminded him of home. Sometimes, the moon edged into the dark, coating outlines with a slight shimmer, so shapes stood out from the darkness. It was in this light he first saw a skinwalker. He watched one of the women walk behind a shed, and then a fox or a foxlike animal appeared. It padded into the trees. He waited for hours, and he never saw the woman reappear.

In these moments, George remembered the stories the old people told. They were stories that he, as a wide-eyed child, believed for all the world to be true. They were stories from the beginning. They were stories of transformation. The stories of witches and skinwalkers, those who go on all fours, told of avenging and nefarious deeds. They were taught to bury their fingernails and hair and to kick dirt over their pee. A skinwalker cursed you, or became you, with the magic of a single clipped finger nail, or a strand of hair. He believed these women, on this other side of the world, had the power to turn into a fox and slip into the jungle forest and leave this world behind. If they had that power what else could they do? He knew better than to doubt his eyes. The next morning, the guys always laughed.

"It ain't nap time out there," they said. "Chief, you've got to quit with that bogey man shit. You're the bogey man. I'm the bogey man. We're the ones people need to fear. We're the bogey men."

They all knew it. The jungle did have the power to change you. In the dark, you were the dark. You were the bogey man. The jungle and the war transformed him, turned him into something out of the old stories.

The next night, he waited again. The same dark wet sludge seeped into his boots, and pants, and shirt. The same leeches attached to his balls. He lay there, a shadow unmoving. He held his breath. Again, like the night before and the night to come he watched those women disappear behind a wall or stand of trees only to slip into the jungle. Did they know he was there?

In the morning, back at the tents, he stripped naked and pulled or burned off the leeches and reported to the guys about the traffic on the road.

"Four groups last night," he grabbed an old newspaper, "and I saw the fox."

They shook their heads and joked with each other about the crazy Indian, but they left him alone with his paper.

The bogey man came home with him. There were no other words for it. The drinking made him argue and arguing made him fight and the fighting turned him into the bogey man and the bogey man made him drink. It was a coil of inevitability. The fighting stopped when his back fused together and after the torrent of beer ended. By then, he and his wife were more strangers than when they first married.

The day he decided he wasn't ready to give up every part of his life was the day he saw it again. He woke early. A dream of falling, high in a forest canopy, left his mind just as he tried to remember it. What made that day different from the blurred days on end before it eluded him? Maybe it was the sun shining into his room after weeks of winter gray, or maybe there had been something to his dream, or maybe his binge ran some natural course. At the time, George did not consider these intricacies, but he would later, as he spent more and more days following tracks in the desert. That morning he pulled off sleep like a cobweb. He stepped out around back to pee. He saw it as he was kicking dirt over the muddy splatter.

It loped just out of sight by the coop, past the old pile of cinder block. He called for his daughter. With his voice low and quiet he called for her. She loved the desert fox.

"Kaila."

She didn't answer. The red fox stopped, black tinged ears perked. It turned as he called for her. There, kicking dirt, groggy from sleep and drink he couldn't remember the last conversation with his daughter. He called her again. The days of her following him everywhere, almost underfoot, ended long ago, but at that moment, with the fox just around the coop, he wished she were there behind him. The fox watched from across the gravel yard as he called her name again. The morning light cast a shadow across the fox's face and the yellow slit eyes looked round and brown.

"Must not be able to hear me," he said to the fox, "or maybe she's not here."

George walked to the chicken coop. The fox's footsteps were ever so light, because he saw no tracks.

As weeks tumbled into months and then years, his companion lingered longer and longer in sight. Was it the same fox traveled across the ocean? Was it the same one after all these years?

Here with rain bands chasing each other along the horizon, sitting under the shrub tree, George saw it again. His Vietnamese fox. Somehow, improbably, here, nine thousand miles from the jungle, was his skinwalker. She followed him some days. Some days she just stayed right out of sight, the flash of a tail slipping behind a rock.

Today, the fox sat upright like a carving of an Egyptian cat. She sat still except for the twitch of an ear. Just for a moment she sat up, and then she hopped into the air landing softly to swat at something on the rock face at her feet.

She toyed with two rattlesnakes. Both tiny snakes shook their preformed rattles without any sound. It was a warning, with a shiver of their tails, to keep back. They were new to the earth and much

11

meaner now than when full grown. Their mamas kicked them out into the world as soon as they were born. George figured baby snakes held a bit of a grudge because of it. He thought of the conversation with his wife early that morning.

"Mean as a snake," George said. They made no noise even though their nubbed tails quivered in warning.

George figured they'd just been born. He moved towards the pair of snakes with slow, quiet footsteps. His toes touched the ground first and then he rolled his foot into the heel and then stepped with the other foot. Slow, deliberate steps, one at a time until he was an arm's length from this coiled pair.

The fox sat on the flat face of the boulder. The worn surface of the rock ran split and pocked like a miniature canyon. She watched George tip-toe to a stop.

"You could make yourself useful," George whispered to the fox. As if on command the fox leaned in to swat, holding her left paw just out of reach.

As he said the words, and the fox swatted, the rattlesnakes moved in opposite directions. The one near George disappeared into a crack at his feet.

"Damn."

The other one struck out at the fox. The snake struck twice. George stayed still with his arms out as if balancing a tightrope. The fox gave a half swat with her paw and then jumped back. She turned off the rock. The snake slipped into the crack like the other one.

They both got away.

"Damn," he said again. First ones he'd seen all day and he let the tiny things slip away. He looked around for the fox. She was gone. A fox was fast, but those strikes were just as fast. He hoped the snake missed.

George wandered the rock slide. He searched the scree pile. He kept an eye out for snakes warming in the sun, but now he scanned the desert around him for the fox. The larger boulders, a set of giant dice rolled to a stop, clumped together. Early in the season, after rattlesnakes left their dens, they only traveled a short distance before staking out a territory. These rock piles warmed all day in the sun. He stopped often, on his way back to the truck, to sit under a shrub tree and watch the desert do the same. He sat and waited and hoped to see the fox. Without a sign of fox or snake, George circled back to his pickup and drove home. He wiped his brow just under the band of his hat. The greedy afternoon collected the heat. The rain bands were still around, but the sun glared between them.

Ropey shadows stretched across the gravel drive. Limbs from the tiny trees by the edge of the gravel rut pointed his way home. Their shadowed twins pointed the same direction as the sun beat down on the trees. The small hop trees huddled together, each trying to hide in the cool shade of the other. One of the shadows turned. A long thick shadow bent at an impossible right angle as if a second sun was shining down on just that one branch from another direction.

George stepped on the brake. The tires locked to a stop, kicking up a cloud of dust. He stepped down from the cab and there lay a beautiful rattlesnake. Five feet long if it was a foot, and dead as dead is. His truck tire almost ripped the body in half as it locked and skidded. The old people would disapprove. Half of the snake whipped around behind the tire, pinned to the ground. The rattle was a good size, so he took out his pocket knife, kneeled down, and cut it off.

"Like cutting off a penis," he said to himself.

He rattled it. It sounded like candies rattling inside a plastic Tic Tac box. He gave it one more shake, before he climbed back into the cab and drove the last bit to the house.

In the yard his aquariums scattered out of place. They were tipped on their sides. George stopped the truck and got out. He glanced in each, prodding with a stick. He looked through every overturned glass tank. He scanned the yard, but all of his snakes were gone. She had done it. Was he angry? There would always be more. He realized there would always be more. They waited under the porch or curled up on the small rafters of the chicken coop. The released snakes would wait, patient after their captivity. George picked his way across the yard toward the pile of cinder blocks. He thought he might be able to find one hiding in a core before it escaped into the desert. Even if they all escaped, he could find more.

The screen door banged open into the side of the house.

"You never let them go!" his wife screamed. Her hair an angry medusa mess whipped around as she turned in the doorway to stare at him. Her eyes were puffy. Her eyes were angry.

"What have you done?" he asked.

"What have you done?" she screamed. She turned into the dark of the house.

His daughter lay prone on the couch.

"Your grandson pushed the lids all morning." She talked slowly. "How many times have I asked for you to get rid of them? How many times has she asked you to get rid of them?"

His daughter lay so still he couldn't see her breathing. Her hair matted to her face. Drops of sweat beaded and dripped to the pillow at her head leaving dark spots like rain in dust. Her bare legs were still. On her arm, a moist poultice of crushed leaves and stems dripped. It was made up of the young tender leaves from sunflowers that lined the edges of their garden and of creeping zinnia and aloe from the herb table by the window.

"How long has it been?" George watched the toddler sitting on the floor by the couch. Chicken Noodle was a quiet child.

"Where were you?" he asked his wife.

"Where were you?" she accused. "Always out looking for those snakes."

George looked at his wife and down at the boy on the floor dragging a stick over the fibers of the floor rug. He kneeled down next to the couch and lifted the poultice. The arm was red and hard. He ran his fingers along the taut skin of his daughter's arm. He turned her palm into the light. It was swollen and dark. The bruising around her hand already split the skin and the blood blisters leaked.

"Kaila." He said her name quietly.

The front door gaped open. The screen door, half open, moved and squeaked. The faint yips and barks of desert coyotes entered into the house. The smell of rain followed on the tail end of those yips.

The barely visible snake bites yellowed her hand. The transformation of her soft smooth skin to the discolored and mummified hand he held sickened him. Twice the snake struck, sinking fangs into the fleshy side of the palm. Along with wrapping the poultice, his wife splinted the arm. That was good. The less it moved the less the venom moved. Blood leaked from burst veins farther up the arm. It was full of venom though. It was too late. She was full of venom now. The way the veins pushed against the skin told George everything he needed to know. It had been hours since the snake struck, and they were hours from town and further even from a clinic. She was already unconscious.

George got up to his feet.

His wife turned black eyes from their daughter onto him.

"The thing is," again he spoke quietly, but then he stopped himself, letting the words float alone into the room.

The sound of rain drummed from overturned aquariums in the yard.

Then he said it, and he didn't mean to say it aloud, "We've got to figure out how to forgive ourselves."

For These Are Wells Without Water

S he rode in at dusk hounded by a nightmare. One hand rested on the horn of her western saddle. The other tucked under her belt, pressed against her stomach. October colored the miles of pasture land in fading light. Tall pines clotted the upper slopes of the valleys. Their branches flashed white bellies in the stronger gusts. The wind and dark turned northern New Mexico into the high plains of some-place else, someplace other than here—some place where thought and memory stretched out forever, a fence with no beginning or end.

Turned in her saddle, she could see the slopes rise under the run of rail and barbed wire until it disappeared into the land. One strand of galvanized wire stretched along the top of the fence she followed all afternoon, and it glinted from time to time in the slowdown of the day. It led into a wide yard with wooden buildings along its edges. The Rancher stood off to the side and watched her turn into the yard. He was a tall man. He stood back on the heels of his boots and kept still while his eyes moved with her into the yard.

"Well, girl, I expected you earlier in the week," he said. His eyes slid with her as she slipped from the saddle. A crow hopped the fence rail behind him. The black feathers of the crow ruffled with another gust.

"Patched a spot of fence. Looked like it'd been cut open. Met some weather too." She nudged a pup away with her boot. The mangy animal hung back and circled around them to a fencepost and lay down. Its fur lifted off in strips, and the irritated skin bumped in a rise of hackles. She coughed to swallow down a rise of bile.

"Didn't find anything?" The Rancher looked at the mud caked to her batwing chaps. A feathery mesquite branch flashed green and fell when her boot stepped from the stirrup. It landed in the dirt and she crushed the tiny leaves when she pivoted towards him. She knew he had already taken an account of the stolen cattle. The horses were on his mind.

"Didn't find anything," she said. "Didn't see another horse out there."

"You said you could wrangle?"

"I told you I ran sheep mostly," she said. "Never did string much."

"Sheep are Navajo business down here." The Rancher spit. "I need a wrangler. You're going to need to show me something."

"Froze into my saddle up in Wyoming for them sheep," she said, "I ain't Navajo. I learn fast." She leaned onto the side of her horse and breathed in and out, deep and steady.

"You okay?"

"It's nothing. A bit of gut rot."

"So you didn't find anything," the Rancher said.

"Tired of freezing stiff to the saddle up there," she said. Her appaloosa stepped in and shook its head. Its ears, high and pointed, flicked a buzzing fly back. Spots ran down the coat of its neck to its underbelly. A twist of thorns barbed into the saddle blanket and she cut them out with an old folding cattle knife.

"It'll catch up with you soon enough here."

"We'll see," she said.

The Rancher leaned back on his heels and rolled his shoulders. "We'll see," he agreed. He nodded toward the stalls. "Juarez and a couple of the boys are earmarking a new bull."

"New bull?"

"For what he is, got it bedrock. Thirteen thousand dollars," said the Rancher, "He's squared off like a tree trunk."

She led the horse and loosed the saddle. She scratched at the swirls of the cow licked hide which was pressed in place from the long ride. She rubbed the sides where the leather strap cinched tight.

"Hola, chica," Juarez grinned. He pulled rope through his hands and coiled it at his feet.

"Still no Español, Juarez," she said. She twisted the tether around her hand with another loop.

"No problema," Juarez said. He turned to the young ranch hand next to him, quickly spoke. Their laughter erupted from a place deep inside of them.

Several other ranch hands across the yard perched on the metal corral fence. Their muddy boots left long tracks of dirt on the steel tubes, and they sat there, on the top, nodding at each other. The wide shoulders of the bull rose and fell. A spray canister broken by the bull's hooves leaked a bluish insecticide into the trample of clumped dirt.

"That's a bull y'all got there," she said.

Juarez grinned. "Mucho grande," He said. His hands came together like he was showing her the size of a fish, and he winked. Juarez looked down at her boots then up her legs to her waist.

"I'm cleaning up," she said. She walked with her horse around the side and felt the stillness of everything, even the bull, watching her leave. Her boot toed the ground, and she stumbled around the corner of the building. The horse followed, ears twitching.

She stepped into the dark of the barn and vomited into the dirt. The foam of her vomit bubbled, soap suds clinging to an empty sink. The green rolled hay smelled sweet and her throat burned. She gagged again and leaned onto the wooden stall planks, her forearm against the wood, and her forehead slid, sweaty, against the skin. Her horse shook his head, clinking the bit, and stretched his pink tongue out to a wisp of hay at the edge of one of the stalls. Tin roof shingles grated and popped overhead.

The next day, red smeared the morning sky. Crows announced the early arrival of two cowboys. The crows flew in from the mountains, and they rode eddies of air, pushed and prodded by the wind, like piles of brush caught up in a flash flood and rolling this way and that.

"Una problema," she heard one of them tell the Rancher.

The Rancher stood in the middle of the lot and leaned into the wind.

They told him they woke up to find one of the horses missing. Half a mile behind. It was dead. Its eyes and tongue cut out.

"Also, la verga," said one of the cowboys. He dangled his pointer finger as he said it. The wag of the finger worked into her memory, an uncovered worm desperate to wriggle back into the safety of the ground. When she was little, her father's big hands came together to clasp his thick fingers in the cave of his palms, and then he lifted the index fingers to peak above the mesa of his knuckles.

Her father said, "Here is the church and here is the steeple, open the doors and see all the people." He then turned his hands up and wriggled all the other fingers.

The wind pushed the sun's heat off of the barn wall—still she shivered and pressed her stomach with the flat of her hand.

"A lion?" asked the Rancher.

"No, no gato," said one of the Mexicans. He was big boned in the face. He hopped down from his horse. "Chupacabra, quizas."

"It ain't no chupacabra. That's just Mexican bullshit, maybe a coyote." The rancher nodded towards the fence post where the pup usually lay.

"No tracks, though," said the other cowboy.

"No tracks?" said the Rancher, "why y'all ride in?"

"Because that's not all. Dos calves missing."

"I guess you found them?"

"Si."

"And what's with them?" asked the Rancher.

"Same mamadas. Same bullsheet," said the big boned Mexican. He curled his upper lip when he said bullshit.

"Same bullshit?"

"Same pinche thing, Jefe. Missing ojos y—" He pointed to his eyes, pretending to cut them out, twisting his wrist in the air. Then he sliced at the air by his ears.

"And no blood," said the other cowboy, "There is no blood."

"Weather come through last night. Might have been lightning up there."

"No. No lightning. Rain and wind, pero no lightning."

"Well, it had to been something, boys."

A week later, the cowboy rode back in to the ranch. "Senorita," he said. He grabbed his hat. She braided a leather strap to her saddle, and her fingers stilled while he passed.

She and the Rancher had been on the shady side of the barn for a better part of the afternoon. She asked him about the chupacabra. It sucked livestock dry of blood. In certain parts, stories were it was both human and dog. Some places it didn't just steal the organs, but the babies, and some places it shifted into any form, into anything.

"Fucking fairytale," the Rancher said. He rubbed his hands on his jeans like he was cleaning his palms.

She didn't ask any more questions, and they didn't speak, just caught up in their own thoughts as the heat of the afternoon collected around them. Tack lay at their feet. Leather straps and stirrups newly oiled glistened wet in the afternoon.

"Banditos again," the cowboy said, "Rustlers made off with twenty more head of cattle."

"Well goddamn it, what do I give you dinero for?" The Rancher tossed a coil of rope into the pile at their feet.

"We see nothing. No oyemos. Nada." He made a squeaky sound with his lips and brought his thumb and forefinger together.

"Well, they're rustling you, ain't they? They ain't going to come up and ask for them are they?" The Rancher kicked a clump of dirt against the barn.

Screams pitched across the yard. The echoing screams pierced the afternoon. They sounded as if they came from every direction. The Rancher stepped away from the barn wall, into the sunlight, and blinked while he turned his head.

"What is that?"

"Pain," said the Rancher. His voice didn't carry far. His voice stayed distant, a whisper.

Cow hands climbed and jumped the fences on the outer corrals and ran into the yard. From around the barn, a young boy slid into view. The dust of the yard lifted into the air.

"Jefe!" The boy kept running across the yard.

"Jefe. The bull."

They followed the boy to the far side of the outer corral.

Juarez leaned on the railing and covered his nose with his hand, and another ranch hand pulled his red bandana up from around his neck.

The eyes of both bull and dam were missing, cored out. The dam's udder cut out. An oval of hide, like a window into the body of the cow, opened up where her udder should be. Two legs and a tail lay next to the pile of intestines. Every cut and disembodied part, even the white ballooned intestines, freed of blood. A precise cut circled the bone of each leg where it had been removed from the body. The heat of the afternoon weighed in with the smell.

The bull was missing his two back legs. The scrotum removed. A clean oval, like the cut for the udder on the dam, is all that remained.

Between the animals, a wad of intestines lay in a pile. In the middle a set of tiny hooves and legs wrapped up in the clear balloon of the uterus.

"Damn, how'd she get with calf?" said the Rancher.

"Is not the bull's calf, Jefe," said the boy, "Is no posible."

"How's that?"

"We've not had him long enough to do that," said Juarez. "Anyway, they not penned together."

"If they've been kept separated, why am I staring at a fucking pile of guts belonging to both of them?"

"No sé. No posible."

"Everything is fucking possible," said the Rancher. "You say this is fucking impossible, but it's looking pretty goddamned possible right now."

"Si, todo es posible." The young ranch hand drug his boot sideways around the cut up bodies. "Lo siento."

"Cut that shit out," the Rancher cussed. "Juarez, you telling me this just went down, in the middle of the day, and no one saw shit?"

Juarez shrugged.

A fly buzzed. The flies were the only creatures sniffing around the bodies. No birds picked the flesh. No tracks or indentions surrounded the animals except for the pit of ground in which each animal sprawled. The fly walked the sticky edge on the dam's stomach.

"Like it's been sucked dry," said the rancher. He cussed under his breath and scratched around his ear. He spat.

"Jefe, chupacabra," said the big boned Mexican.

"Well shit," said the Rancher, "we got us a real life fairy tale then don't we? When we find out, I guarantee it won't be that shit. We got rustlers stealing cattle from one end, this shit happening on the other end, so we'll focus on what we can control. Rustlers can be caught."

"They know where we move the cattle."

"I know," said the Rancher, "they know, but they'll get what's coming to them."

Late that night, her door opened. Branches knocked the back corner in the nighttime wind and she didn't move, already awake. In the dark she heard the hinges whine with the weight of the wood. The outline of shoulders stepping through the doorway blended into the dark of the room and disappeared against the wall. A boot step scuffed the floor. The door squeaked back into place and settled with a bump in its frame. She held her stomach with a hand and gripped her pocket knife with the other.

The slow boot steps across the floor thudded in the way the thud of a giant heart pumped blood through the walls of her room.

She closed her eyelids. The mattress sank with the weight of the man. He sat on the edge of the bed. Once upon a time, her mother sang to her, sitting like that.

"Been a few weeks. How you feeling?" The whisper rumbled with the deep baritone of a voice that didn't often whisper.

"Like shit," she said.

"Still getting sick?" The man leaned in as he spoke. His breath curled heavy around her, like smoke. An old scar cut into his lip pulled the skin tight under the dark stubble of his chin. His hands folded in his lap.

"Yes."

"You decide anything yet?"

"Going to keep it." She put both hands on her stomach. The steel of the cold knife pressed cold against her.

"You showing?" he asked. The branch at the back of the building clawed across the back wall.

"Don't think so."

"Not yet then. How long now?"

"Two months, maybe three."

They breathed together in the dark for a moment. She kept her hands on her stomach and gripped her pocket knife.

"Well, you'll figure it out, I guess," he said.

"I guess," she said. She wondered why she wanted to please the Rustler. Her imaginary friend from her childhood. She believed his whispered instructions, and she always did them. Didn't he always protect her? Did she really believe in him? He told her to leave Wyoming. Told her to leave her father. He even picked out the ride for her to hitchhike. The man in the station wagon was drunk, and he wore black sunglasses even though it was dark when he picked her up off the side of the road. She wanted to believe this was supposed to happen, even when he pulled off the road and parked. Even when his hand groped her, and even when he pulled out his cock, and even after the man crawled off her and began driving again, even then she wanted to believe in the meaning, the reason of a greater cause. The Rustler was, after all, always there for her, always watching out for her.

"What section of fence you working next?"

"They lost a big stud bull today. Six mutilations this month."

"A bull?"

"Thirteen thousand dollar yearling."

He whistled. "Been out to stud?"

"Don't think so. They were just marking it."

"Well damn." He leaned his weight, and the bed groaned and shifted.

"The Mexicans think it's some animal, goat sucker, chupacabra." She pushed her body back from the edge of the bed. The divot his weight made sucked her towards him.

The wind knocked something heavy into the outside wall. They held their breath. The darkness surrounded them.

"Those're stories," he said.

She nodded in the darkness.

"What fence you working next?" he said.

"The valley up towards the forest, just north of here, has a stretch of fence broken up with fallen pine. We're going to fence that section and move the cattle into that valley south of it."

"Then what?"

"Nothing. 'Set up and wait for rustlers this time,' is what he said. He's got us strapping for real. Ain't worth it now. Should have already moved on."

The man reached out and tapped her chest with a thick finger. "Well, that ain't your call," he said. He lowered the hand down her shirt and flexed his fingers into the soft skin under her ribcage. "This better not get in the way. They need to think you're here to work for them, but that's it. When the time comes, you'll let me know."

After the door shut and she heard nothing for a while, she stood up. She wondered if he meant her baby, but she knew he didn't. She was here, waiting. She was his eyes and ears. Something inside her recognized him as other, but although she tried, she could not explain it.

As a child her father said, "Getting a bit old for imaginary friends, aren't you?"

"He talks to me every night," she argued. She didn't understand why her father didn't understand, why he didn't care.

As she got older, he was with her, whispering instructions and manipulations, warning her away. She thought he protected her from older boys or wild willed cattle running in their pens. Still, her father had no patience for what he called *those stories*.

"Don't take to being lied to," he said when she tried to tell him about the devil in her room.

It wasn't until she was much older, until she finished with school, she realized no one else ever saw him. No one else could see him. This devil was like Jesus. She believed in one and her father believed in one. There was a time when her dreams pushed into her thoughts and she remembered foreign memories, memories from some other life, but as she shed sleep and tried to hold onto the images, she could only remember the sound of bird song, or the smell of a faint ocean breeze, or the comfortable feel of the memory itself. That time ended as well, and all she was left with was this thing, this person who guided her, mostly, into safety.

With a hand on her stomach, she walked to the door. Her shirt hung to her knees. She floated across the room. Pressure on her bladder pushed her out of bed often. She stepped outside, and a rip of pain fell out of her body. She dropped forward onto her arms, her pocket knife falling into the dirt. Her stomach clinched and contracted. She grabbed it with both of her hands, leaned forward, hunched over herself.

She reached between her thighs and her fingers slid on sticky skin. Dark blood clots stuck between her thighs. The clots were big, like eggs, and they slipped to the dirt. Her stomach pulled tight and a new rush of blood dropped from her. The weak light hid the most of it, but she could see the stain spread across the hem of her shirt. Like flies hovering around dead cattle, a smell surrounded her. It rose up like just before a late afternoon shower tossed the smell of desert rock back down to earth, and it clung to her, ocean water filling her nose with the salty, sea-air memory from her childhood.

Only one time, as a child, she swam in the ocean.

"It's a gulf, not an ocean," said her father.

The salt air rose from the water. It floated between the wooden buildings in the Texas town. She could smell it. Her skin chafed. She hated it. She was okay rocking in the waves, didn't feel the chafing when submerged, but every movement out of the water was miserable.

"You'll turn into a prune," said her father. He sat, all day, with a long fishing pole jammed into the beach. Every morning, he dug through the loose sand, past the layers of white until the walls of the hole were gray and moist. It is where he kept the beer he drank, covered with a towel.

She splashed in the shallows anyway, near the shore, floating face down in the warm water like the brown beer bottles her father tossed into the surf. The difference was they could hold their breath forever, floating just below the surface. In the deeper spots, still near the beach, where waves played out the last of their energy she pulled her legs up and held them tight and let herself rock. She held her breath. Her long hair floated free around her, the tentacles of a jellyfish bobbing to the will of the current. She wished she could hold her breath forever and stay face down in the warm water too—float away on the current like an empty bottle.

While teaching herself to keep her eyes open under the yellow surface, plops spiraled around her. The weight of little objects landed on her back. Sitting up out of the water, she caught her father grinning, throwing chop from the bucket at his feet high into the air above. All around her tiny fish with nubbed fins, tiny cut up fish without heads, tiny fish heads with no fish bodies rained into the waves. The slime and streaks, the falling fish bits, trailed down her arms and stank for days, no matter how much she scrubbed.

Even after she screamed and ran out of the water, her father kept laughing.

"You should see your face," he kept saying.

She wouldn't swim again.

In the dirt, a tiny fetus lay with its budded limbs blunted, a gray piece of fish bait. It was the size of a man's thumb. Trails of sticky patches on her skin felt funny. The red plush of blood vessels glistened gray. Everything bathed in blood and dirt, and the image of the fetus stayed projected in her mind even when she looked away. It was already a formed memory, like all those fish parts floating around her in the shallows of the Gulf of Mexico.

She closed her eyes. She could still see the nubbed arms. She turned in the muck of her blood and felt for her knife. The sticky handle folded away from the blade. The cover of night lifted across the horizon. The faint morning light stabbed at her eyes. She shut them tight. The darkness lifted too soon, so she lifted the blade to her face and stuck the tip into her eye. She twisted the knife and freed the eyeball from the socket. She gouged out the other eye, and fell backwards onto the ground, covered, once again, in darkness.

Her scream hung close to the ground. It barreled through the doors and windows of the buildings. The shifting wind pulled through the compound carrying her cries.

Large hands pulled her back and held her tight. The Rancher kneeled down in the blood and dirt. He pulled her to him.

"Girl, girl," he said. One of his hands cradled her head to his chest, to the steady thump of his heart. Blood wept from her eye sockets. Her fingertips found the sticky trails running down her cheeks.

The pocket knife lay open on the ground.

She heard Juarez say, "Dios mío."

The weight of a blanket curled over her legs. She wanted to believe in mystery, in meaning. There was no mystery. No meaning. These were the basic truths. Like a good father, hope didn't exist. Like imaginary ones, friends were hard to find. Like preachers claiming rebirth, miracles were empty beer bottles sinking beneath the swell.

The smell of leather, the gold printed cover of her father's bible, pressed in close. The salty air of the ocean swept everything else away, while song birds called to each other, guiding each other into daybreak. Her world stayed the same, insulated with the dark.

She heard him say, "For we wrestle not against flesh and blood."

The Men with Painted Faces

Arise of toothy mountains, the overgrown remains of some ancient dragon, peak into the blue Vietnamese sky and disappear far to the north following sharp slopes and valleys. In front of the mountains, a group of thatched structures on wooden platforms edge the sea of elephant grass leaning with the wind. The blades turn their yellow tops. The wind pushes eddies in the grass from the stilt houses toward the men of the long range patrol waiting in the humid shade, and the smell of tobacco swirls in on top of the gust.

"Damn it, Rub, put that lucky out."

"Need some action." Rub blew smoke out of his nose, venting a dragon's furnace.

"That's the gig, you dumb shit."

George snatched the cigarette out of Rub's mouth and killed it, twisting it in the ground.

"I swear to God, Indian, you piss me off." Rub tapped another cigarette from his crumpled soft pack of Lucky Strikes.

"We're all eat up with mosquito, and whatever else is crawling around, but we will see this through. You will not light that cigarette," hissed Sergeant Rolle. He whispered the command, but the force behind the words, the stare pushing out of the Sergeant stilled Rub.

Rub laughed. "Well shit fellas, if you're going to be like that." He racked the cigarette back into the pack.

Rub never laughed because something was funny.

George didn't need the warning. He leaned back to the papery bark of the spruce trunk.

The men with George prairie-dogged, their backs straight, heads up. They scanned one side of the field to another. It reminded him of home. But these men didn't bark in warning like ground squirrels standing guard at the mouths of their dens. The river of grass distracted the wind catching it, leaning this way and that. The flanks of grass glinted like a school of basa fish and rolled in unison with the oppressive humidity before the afternoon rain.

The men waited so long George felt rooted to the tree, and the other three men transformed into new forest shoots, and time beat like the distant snap of the far off flag fighting in the wind.

The mission was to pick up the Viet Cong informant, bring him out of the mountains.

The blood-filled body of a tick popped between thumb and forefinger. Hours of creeping under double canopy and the four man patrol stopped again in the high valley. They sat at the edge of a fresh clearing cut into the side of the mountain. The clearing stretched—a charred scar, a fresh wound. The hill tribes burned land to expand their crops. On the other side of the new clearing, the sea of grass continued to slither. George rubbed his thigh picking at the head of the tick cemented into his skin. Like stunted tick-covered junipers in the heat of an Arizona summer, the Vietnam jungle swarmed with movement. Ticks swayed in ambush holding out front legs while hind legs surfed the broad backs of jungle leaves. The old junipers on the reservations back home looked alive after a hatching, almost swirling, active like the haze of heat rising from the sun baked desert floor.

One of his grandfather's horses had brushed into an infested shrub on the day of the fire. The horses pulled the body of a tribal elder into the flats of the desert. George's grandfather untethered the tick-covered horse from the sled and shot it through the brain.

"The dead resent us anyway. If we send him into the after with a swarm of ticks they will send that swarm back to us," his grandfather said. He nodded at the wrapped body on the sled.

"What do they resent?" George asked.

His grandfather dragged his heel into the dirt. He picked up a fat-bodied tick and squeezed it. "Our blood," he said. He wiped his fingers clean in the dirt.

"Do the dead not remember we are family?"

"Their world has changed. It can be a dark place, a hard place, a place of suffering."

Tree frogs chorused. Their chirps rose and fell like the chest of a water buffalo struggling through the deep muck of the rice fields. Above his head, a mantis fluttered its wings and landed on his knee. What was Vietnam then? The crawling, the creeping, the darkness—it was all alive with movement haunting the dead world from the muck and wet of this place. In it, all the ticks, backward-spined vectors, hunted George. All the men burned leeches from their balls and their armpits. They followed the blood stains bleeding out of their clothes. George attracted the other vampires, the other blood suckers. He picked them off every day and itched the irritated skin pocked here and there with the leftover disembodied heads burrowed into it, all over his arms and legs. Sometimes when he cored the head of a tick out of his arm with the point of his bowie knife, George noticed a fox creep into his periphery. Its purple hide melded with the shadows. George stopped gouging and lifted his hair from his eyes, but the animal was gone.

The other men never saw it. "Ticks are fevering your brain, Chief," they mocked. Or he was just dismissed. "Fucking Indian."

They had left the infested horse bleeding out into the tumbling sands. How long did the tiny hunters suck on the dead flesh? How long before they crept to higher ground and waited, arms outstretched, for the warm blooded to cross their paths?

Once at the burial grounds, the men covered their arms and faces with white ash. The ash caked around their eyes and the corners of their mouths. It was important to be the face of the dead. The dry heat of the afternoon wicked away their sweat, so the ash didn't leave

31

their faces streaked. Instead, it puffed and settled as the men worked, while the sun dropped behind the mesa to the west. They laid the body flat into a crevice, as shadows stretched from rocks and spires around them. George built the fire. With it, they burned the wooden sled and the stretcher branches and brush used to sweep away their tracks. With footprints swept away, the dead elder would have a hard time following them home, would hopefully never follow them home. George broomed the branches, back and forth, and cleared a swath away from the body like a ray of sun. He swept a path until a half circle of rays in the sand bloomed out from where the body lay in the sandstone.

At the burial site, his grandfather shot the remaining sled horses. The bullet lodged in their skulls, and their knees buckled them to the ground. The grunts the horses made, on their way down, lodged in George's mind like another one of his grandfather's bullets. They belonged to the dead elder and were left behind so he could ride them away. The team of ghost-horses was the last gift from the family and more a gesture of release than a good deed. Another relative placed jars and beads at dead elder's feet and put a knife at his side. The smoke burned their eyes, but no one spoke, and when George cleaned the last set of footprints, he fed the branches to the fire, and the tiny group of men turned their backs to the caverned walls and walked away into the desert.

The old elder's hogan burned last. It was an old, weather-worn structure. The adobe roof ran with cracks like desert rock. The timber sides lost the packed mud years ago and the logs bleached white in the sun, a pile of bones picked clean with time. One more fire before the night was finished. Then, the dead elder would be given way, no longer anchored to the mesas of the southwest. One more fire to set him free and finish the ritual of life to dust.

George followed his thoughts like firelight spreading into darkness, a bright flicker illuminating for a moment the walls of his memories, and then pulling back, a dimming fire retreating from the cover of night.

He rubbed his thumb over the white gas can in the foreground of the picture, forever still, like the burning monk next to it. Ink smudged under his finger into a crease of the paper and then spider webbed into the fibers of the newspaper around the crease. The damp paper smelled sweet. The picture dulled out of focus more every day as George unfolded it and folded it back. The car behind the angry coil of fire sat with its hood open, a mouth wide with wonder. The fire whipped. Even caught still in a photograph, the flames, active and alive, clung to the monk and worked their way around, like the many arms of some angry god still not pleased with the sacrifice.

The clipped newspaper picture dipped and hung limp over his fingers. George cut it out while still stateside. President Kennedy said, "Jesus Christ," when first handed the morning newspaper with the image of self-immolation. George didn't say anything when he held the paper with the burning monk, but he thought about little Earl Tsosie. He folded the clipping into a square and tucked it back into his shirt pocket. He should have pushed Earl away. He should have kicked him back into the night like one did with an annoying puppy. His family moved into New Mexico from the shame he brought them. Fire changed things. At nineteen George volunteered for Vietnam. Nine months later he volunteered to be a front scout with the rangers. He fought to erase his shame, fought for good in this war. For almost a year he slipped into the shadows and back out with the men of his long range patrol. They watched, mostly.

George wiped sweat from his temple. His fingers smudged the black and green grease they smeared on their faces. The grease didn't keep the mosquitoes and bugs from biting their faces and necks and arms, but it dulled the sweat on their skin so they didn't reflect light hiding under the canopy of the jungle, so when the men of the long range patrol stood still they disappeared into undergrowth.

Earl Tsosie was too young for the burial ceremony. Always underfoot, though, he followed George like a hound. At the wooden hogan the older men set bundles of tied grass along the five walls. After lighting fire to the bundles they left George to feed the fire through the night.

"Can someone else tend the flames?" George asked. "I want to join the men."

"Only family members can tend the dead. And you are not old enough to be with the men."

"What about Earl?"

"Little Tsosie's too young to tend a fire."

"He has been following us. He's somewhere here."

"He is too young."

"But it's a big hogan. It will burn long into the night."

"And you will watch it burn long into the night."

George took a long stick, like a shepherd's staff, to tend the fire. He slammed the butt of it into the ground when he was alone. That is when Earl, waiting in a ditch for the older men to leave, climbed to his feet. His face white with ash, the boy grinned. He held George's hand. His tiny fingers squeezed the index finger they wrapped around.

"I painted my face," Earl said to George, "Let me tend. You can ceremony and come back in the morning."

George bit the inside of his lip and twirled the stick in his hands. "Nobody will know."

George handed the staff to Earl. "Somebody always knows," he said, "Take care, hide in the morning light, and I will be back for you then."

George walked to the edge of the fire light and turned. Earl teased the bundles of grass with the long staff. The staff was twice as long as the young boy. George turned into the darkness.

All night they walked through the loud thrum of insects and tree frogs. He saw the fox again. The air felt sticky at the foot of the mountains. Green jungles tangled together walling off every direction. The strangler figs still grew here on the rise out of the coastal jungles. The knobbed roots threw shadows, silhouettes of faces and many-limbed bodies, into the leaves around them, even in the middle of the day. Spirit trees guarded the hill tribes. Trees, great and small, imbued with a family's ancestors were the ghost stories soldiers told each other back at camp. The trees came alive—they killed men. There were stories of soldiers, after questioning some family, dropping dead at the foot of the family's home. There were stories of roots gutting the stomach of a soldier taking a piss. The stories grew at camp and the men laughed. Joints and beers and the camp tents dulled their wide-eyed feelings to the animism. Out in the forests and jungles, the stories were not repeated. Instead of swapping stories, they stayed quiet and sipped water at every stop. All day long, water poured off of them, and they drank and drank and drank. The water the men forced down at camp beaded off their skin into their shirts and hung, wet and heavy, as they sweat it out in the helicopter that dropped them into the carcass of the old French fort. It sat midway up the mountain, a short respite before the fight for footing up the steep slopes began. Even as the helicopter blades smacked through the air, still audible in the distance, George tasted the cotton of dehydration on the tip of his tongue.

Images of bonfires and celebration flickered in his mind. The deliberate steps of a forest fox caught his attention and interrupted his memory. Leaves swayed in place of the fox next to the glisten of a line running just off the ground a step in front of them. George held up his hand. He pointed his chin to the stake mine.

"Standard," Sergeant Rolle said, "get up here. George found himself the cutest fucking little bouncing betty I've ever seen."

Private Standard eased the line in his hands following it slowly with his fingertips.

Rub spoke up, distracted by something in the forest canopy. "Don't want to hear about that fox shit again," he said.

"Not making it up," George said.

"Don't give a shit, tired of your five-year-old, nursery rhyme bull-shit," Rub said. "You found another one. Good for you. That's why you run point. A little luck and your superstitious ass will trip one soon. I'm tired of following an Indian around."

George stopped. He hunched down under the waxy leaves of the fruit trees and pointed his bowie knife at Rub. "Nursery rhymes are what your schools teach little white girls and boys."

"Fuck you, George," Rub said. Rub laughed. He tapped the tree he leaned on with the barrel of his rifle. Specialist Jimmy Rub carried the long barreled bolt action Winchester. The only time George saw a calm Rub was when he was sighting through the scope of that rifle. Rub called the mountains of Western North Carolina home. The young sniper never got mail from home and only once did he mention the rolling pastures of the southern Appalachians. In slow moments, George whispered the word Appalachian to himself. He said it like Rub, slow and lazy. Appalachian.

"A thousand more won't change one misplaced step," George said. He stared at Rub. The tall man walked the hillsides with nervous energy. He liked to stay hidden. They all liked to stay hidden. In the shadows of undergrowth, they disappeared. Their greased skin let the white of their eyes escape, but everything else stayed camouflaged and hidden, like all the other creepers and crawlers of the undergrowth.

"You're just a fucking useless redskin. We're grown ass men out here. Get your eyes off me," Rub said. "When he finishes with that line," Rub nodded at Standard, "you get us up this mountainside, until then you can leave me the fuck alone."

George skidded down the leafy slope and drove his shoulder into Rub's stomach. The two men landed on the ground and slid and rolled down the steep slope.

"You stop calling me a redskin," George hissed.

Their legs and arms wrapped around each other and they fell. Farther and farther down the slope they rolled until the wide base of a fig stopped their descent. George rolled on top of Rub. He pinned one arm to the ground. Rub's other arm pinned itself underneath him.

George punched. His fist landed in the middle of Rub's face. He battered the man who was closed up, hunched behind his hands and arms. After the last punch thudded out into the trees, George rolled over and sucked air into his lungs.

Rub laughed. "Is that all you got, pussy?"

George stood and leaned into the hill. The clouds settled right above their heads. Wisps of white pulled at their eyes. The forest stilled.

"Shut up," George whispered. He pointed around them in a circle and held a finger to his lips.

"You fuckers done?" Sergeant Rolle yelled.

"Shh," George shushed under his breath. The two men up the bank were only voices, swallowed by the fog.

A crackle. A footstep. A settling branch. Some noise caught up in his mind like a radio signal attracting antennas. Tiny hairs on the back of George's neck stood on end.

Rub's nose flowed blood. He pressed the top of his wrist under his nose and pointed with his other hand at the trunk of another strangler fig. The roots of that tree climbed and sloped like a mini version of the mountains of Vietnam. George stepped to the back side and Rub crawled to the front. The ever so wide tree trunk could hide all four men of their patrol. George nodded to Rub. They circled around the opposite direction of the tree trunk.

A young boy sat back on his heels with his head down and his hands up. George examined the trees around them. He listened for something, the sound of things out of place, but he couldn't hear anything.

"Well shit, we got us a little sneak," Rub said.

George heard Sergeant Rolle and Specialist Standard sliding down to them.

"I tell you what," Rub said, "you little gook." He kneeled down grabbed the boy's black hair with one hand and pulled his other hand across the neck.

George didn't see the knife, but a line spread across the tiny neck and the boy's dark eyes got wide, so wide the white stood out. Cattle rolled their eyes like that when they struggled in the muddy waters of spring.

Rub grinned at George. He held the Bowie out handle first. "You dropped your knife."

George kneeled down. He held the kid's still warm hand in his own. The eyes were not wide anymore. George put a hand in his hair. "You fuck," he whispered.

Sergeant Rolle cussed, but it didn't matter.

"Fuck, Rub," Standard said. "That's a Montagnard. He isn't Viet Cong. He isn't even Vietnamese."

"Who else you think ran that wire?" Rub said. He looked down at the slumped body and kicked it over. "They all look the same anyway."

George grabbed Rub and pushed him against the tree. "You fuck," he said again.

"Let it go," said Sergeant Rolle, "Let's go."

How could he let it go? Another slender body at his feet. Another young boy in the wrong place. Another mistake reminding George of all his failures.

Flat on his belly, George had listened to the men sing long into the night. In the gray of morning George pushed away into a ditch and checked on Earl Tsosie.

The burnt hogan spit smoke into the air. The heavy adobe roof fell into the burned out structure. One wall buckled.

"Earl." George waited, but heard nothing. "Earl, wake up."

George kicked the burning clumps back against the Hogan and the elders returned. One of them picked up a charred Shepard's hook.

"George, we burn this last."

"I know," said George. He walked the edges of the flat, but Earl was not hiding in a ditch.

"Why did you burn it?" The elder with the staff pulled at the fallen timber wall.

"George."

"Yes."

"Were you alone all night?"

"Yes."

The staff hooked some cloth and the elder pulled. A pocket opened in the coal and the stink of burned flesh overwhelmed the char of wooden ember in the air. A tiny hand rolled over. The fingers black and cracked like the rock of desert spires. The fingers curled. The men pried the fallen timber off of the tiny body. Earl's father dropped to his knees and looked at the boy's hand. It lay there, pointing. The man turned his head and looked at George.

"What shame is this?"

The burnt arm split open. It split like the meat of an animal on a spit. George struggled with that smell, the memory of burnt flesh. He still woke to it.

"What shame!" yelled Earl's father, "What shame!"

In a gust, the elephant grass shuttered memories. "Chief, lead out," said Sergeant Rolle. He stood there like one of the Dragon Spruce at their backs. He always leaned, comfortable in his space, like he belonged, like a tree on a mountain slope.

"We should wait," Rub said. His low voice carried just far enough for George to hear it over the moving grass. The grass picked up its slither with the wind dropping in from the far off mountain range.

"Let's go."

"We been sitting here," said Rub, "not a single thing has moved."

"He's right. No chickens, goats, kids."

Sergeant Rolle pushed on his chin until his neck cracked and then nodded for George to start walking.

"Man, that mine strung way up here in the mountain. That kid sneaking around us. Something ain't right." Rub stared at George.

"Let's go now. We wait too long and we'll piss away our chance."

"Ho Chi Minh trail is just south of here. If we aren't careful, we won't have a chance to piss away," said George, "It's the supply line south we need to worry about, not some out of place mine."

"George is right," said Sergeant Rolle, "Charlies crawling all around."

"George is never right," said Rub.

Something was off, but they had sweated in this spot for long enough. That was the thing about humidity—after a while, it made you dumb. It crept into your senses and gummed them up. George strapped his M-16 to his vest. His pack stretched on his shoulders, and he stepped from the edge of the forest down into the moving sea of grass. Slaps. A flutter of fabric. A flag in wind led them across the field. The man they were searching for wouldn't be there. The blades of grass tickled and itched. They dropped down into the boggy area of the field. They walked single file. The green and yellow stalks blotted out the world.

Thin red flags moved at the far edge of the plot. On skinny white poles they turned in the wind, playful. A large tualang tree towered above them. It was the only tree in the cleared valley. A giant wandered down from the mountain slopes. It stood sentry.

"Big tree," said Standard.

Sergeant Rolle laughed.

Standard kept his eyes on the tree. The flags snapped warning.

A tiny man stepped out of a doorway. He didn't wear the brown khakis the men in the cities wore. His embroidered clothes ran with colors.

"Damn it, fucking Montagnards." Rub turned his head and stared at George. "Fucking natives."

Standard stepped forward and greeted the tiny man. "Xin chào."

The tiny man spoke a lilting jumble of vowels.

Standard replied to the small man, and then he shrugged. "Don't know Sergeant. He don't speak Vietnamese," he said.

They walked into the dark house. The elderly man sat on the floor with his family.

"Fuck it," said Rub, "At least we have something to do while we wait." He yanked a flat spoon from a young girl. "Might as well enjoy ourselves. We came all this way after all." The long-haired girl looked across the room to her mother, or grandmother. Rub dipped the spoon in the big stew pot.

"Leave them alone, Rub."

"This is bullshit. All we do is creep. Get all the way up here and the fucker isn't here?"

"So we wait," said George.

"Someone here knows something," said Rub.

"What are they going to know? They're not part of this war."

"Standard, ask them again."

The Montagnards sat on a worn rug at the side of a low table. Their faces blanked without expression in the low light of the room.

George grabbed Rub's shoulder.

"Get off me, Chief."

"Leave this family alone."

"Get your hands off of me."

"Get out of here," said George. He pushed toward the doorway.

"We'll set up over there and wait until morning," Sergeant Rolle said. He pointed at the family. He pointed out the doorway. The family looked back, still and silent.

George pushed Rub out, and the Sergeant nodded to the family one more time and dropped the door cloth behind him. "Jesus, Rub, what is wrong with you?"

"Nothing's wrong with me."

"This ain't the Wild West."

"You seen where we are?" Rub said. He pointed the spoon at George. "It is the Wild West. Natives need to be taught a lesson."

"Rub."

"Oh fuck that. We've been dumped into a nightmare, and you're calling me off like a dog? We're fucking bogey men."

"Straighten up, Rub." Sergeant Rolle said.

"Whatever."

"We got some bad intelligence. It happens. You know that. Ain't no excuse for the shit you're pulling."

George listened to them argue. He rested his head back onto the wall. Rub had it right. All the creeping and darkness in the world piled up here. They were supposed to make sense of it. His thumb worked a knot from his thigh.

Rub bitched. Sitting at the wooden doorway, he pulled his shirt up and squeezed black blood from a leech dangling in his armpit hair.

George closed his eyes. Just for a moment, he told himself. The sound of the grass in the wind faded with Rub's grooming. Sounds lifted and traveled out of the room. A fox sat still in the center of the room, or his mind. Rub, Standard, and Sergeant Rolle vanished. A gray light carried the smell of burnt skin. The smell of memory. The fox departed.

Screams yanked him awake. He jumped to his feet, gun in his hands. The shadows in the room wavered. The clearing flooded bright with yellow light. The darkness slunk far into the grassy fields and up the steep banks surrounding them.

The family's house roared and cracked and fire twisted along beams and rolled like a cloud, a thunderhead, moving forward. Rub stood in front of the burning building with his arms crossed. The cloth doorway hidden from view. The entrance blocked by piled high fire wood. The wood stacked so deep it would be too heavy to push aside. The snaps of the wood grew with the height of the fire.

The entire clearing around them lit like day, and the smoke towered far above them at the tip of the great flame. It was the screams that brought George to his feet and the screams that kept them now rooted to the ground. A low hiss seeped out of the fire, but over the hisses and the snaps the pitch of the screams from inside melded together. Earl Tsosie must have screamed. Earl had been asleep too. Did the smoke and fire overwhelm him before the searing pain cut into his every nerve ending? George pulled his t-shirt away from his body. It was heavy. This family woke from sleep too, yet the fire did not let them go quietly into the night. Their shrieks cried out. Those screams revised his memory, forever changed him. For when he closed his eyes, it was Earl Tsosie who screamed in the darkness. Earl's screams continued in unending agony and sleep tore itself forever from George's grasp. Here, among the tiny crawling insects in the wet jungles and foggy mountains men became monsters and their futures dimmed, blinking away the screams of the past. Rub was right. They were bogey men. They were born anew.

Standard asked God for help. Standard stared at the giant tree. The waver of fire light moved around its branches and shadows shifted in the flicker. Faces molded and rendered on its knobs and bark with the orange fire light. The wind, the never ending wind, twisted sound down from the mountains. Voices, many voices, joined the screams and the fire grew, its fingers reaching high above the tree.

A storm pushed the valley from one end to the other. Stagnant air sank into the darkness.

Rub looked up into the sky. He stepped back from the twisting tree, from the ancient voices settling into the valley. A long shadow cast off his shoulders to George's feet.

George stepped backwards as well, out of the shadow to the edge of the light. The tall tree continued to move in the flickering of flame. George turned his back to the burning scene. He crouched through the leaves into the humid undergrowth. He sat cross legged and straight backed. He cupped his hands together in his lap. He catalogued memory. It drifted in the air, the smell of burnt ember and flesh.

The Dead Indian

Curtis slumped down on the floor. The trailer door tapping into its frame. He sat up against the wall. The floor shined, bare and clean. His unbuckled pants sagged around his legs and his cold ass stuck to the linoleum.

After a shower and half a beer, Curtis left for work. Struggling to free itself from a long rusted nail, white and pink striped underwear fluttered in the wind. It hung on the fencepost at the end of the yard. The drive down the dirt road started in the gray of early morning. The wide open sky stretched with clouds. Snowflakes driven by the wind erased the far off mountains. He drove to Larry's gas station.

"Morning, Curtis," Larry said. His large shoulders and chest squeezed behind the counter.

"Larry."

The orange mud of spring time desert discolored the white floor. Curtis followed a path of smeared boot prints to the glass doors at the back and then back up the counter.

Larry smiled. "You look a party went long."

"Look like I feel then." Curtis pointed for a pack of cigarettes.

"Alma showed last night late," Larry said, "asked to phone."

"She did?"

"Looked to me she'd been walking a bit. Her brother picked her up." Larry slid the pack of cigarettes across the wooden countertop.

"He did?"

Larry nodded, "Starting early?" He pressed his lips and pointed his chin at the twelver of Schlitz on the counter.

"Buying early," Curtis pulled his black coat open showing the badge pinned over his heart on the blue button up shirt, "Got to work first."

"That what you call riding around in that truck?"

"And you're not sitting on your ass?"

"You see Alma last night?" asked Larry.

"What do you mean?" Curtis smelled the overdone dogs in their steam rollers. He tasted the stale beer he finished earlier.

"Just a question," said Larry.

"Why can't y'all just be happy?" Curtis rubbed his chin and his lip.

"We are happy enough. Would you be happy in forced poverty?"

"No one's forcing anything," Curtis said. He stopped rubbing his jaw and put the pack of cigarettes in his coat pocket.

"Curtis, the reservation's got real problems."

"Give me a break."

"We fight to live like a third world country surrounded entirely by a first world country."

"Real third world countries would be happy to switch with you."

"Curtis, you should come with me to Albuquerque on Friday. The Kiva Club has a meeting. These issues need our focus. Alma would love to have you there."

"Jesus, more Kiva Club. That's all Alma's been talking about. Why can't y'all just be happy?"

"We ain't going anywhere, Curtis," said Larry.

"Well, Larry, neither are we." Curtis grabbed his beer. He held the door for a Navajo girl who looked down at her dirty tennis shoes as she walked through the door. Her braids pulled down across her ears and Curtis could see white of scalp under dark brown hair.

The gray skies lifted and wind pushed the odd flurry along the border toward Colorado. The call to be on the lookout came across all radio channels, "Possible hostage situation. Suspect. Navajo male."

Since the Wounded Knee incident began, activists across the Indian nation pushed for recognition. The Indian Nation was unhappy, and Curtis, having grown up on a border town to a reservation, having met Alma in high school, felt torn. It felt like a rancher shooting sick cattle in the head. The cattle might pull through, but they might make others sick.

Curtis cut through the grocery parking lot and pulled the truck out of gear. He grabbed the shotgun from the back window of his pickup and ran across the street. The pickup rolled to a stop on the flat parking lot. The driver door left open.

"Where you been," asked his partner. He kneeled at the back corner of a white Impala station wagon. The street stretched away from them in two directions. Parked cars lined one side and the box buildings scrolled along with their store fronts, the big glass windows reflecting everything—a parallel world busied itself alongside this one.

"Hauling ass to get here. Where is everybody?" said Curtis.

"You been drinking?"

"No. Where is everybody?"

"You and Alma getting into it again?" asked the officer, still kneeling. He took his eyes off the storefront across the street and nodded at the cut lip.

"Leave it alone. Who bagged the mayor?" Curtis rubbed at his lip.

"She isn't right for you, you know?"

"Well, what do you know?"

"Some kid dragged him out of his office down the street. Decided to hole up in there." His partner pointed across the street at one of the big store front windows. "All I know is, how long you going to keep fucking that bitch?"

"What happened? And it's none of your business."

"I don't know everything. He pulled in front of town hall in a pickup and pulled a body out of the back onto the sidewalk."

"Well shit. What body? Dead?" Curtis turned his head up the street toward town hall.

"Don't know. It won't work out. If you're honest, Curtis, you know it hasn't been working out."

"I don't want to talk about it."

The door at the store front slammed open.

"Look at him shag ass," said his partner. A young man moved from the front door with short quick steps. His dark hair hung around his face. His jeans dirty.

"Hey," yelled Curtis. He stood up and rounded the back of the Impala into the middle of the street.

"Curtis. Easy."

"Stop walking." Curtis yelled. "Don't move!" He crossed the street to the sidewalk. His shotgun pointed down.

Curtis recognized the man's boots first as the soles scratched and turned on the sidewalk. With the pivot, kernels of rock salt crushed like gravel under a tire.

"Don't move!" Curtis yelled. Sam Lamont twisted around at the sound of Curtis' voice. They focused on the other. Sam's hand came around his body and Curtis saw a cigarette between the fingers.

"I said don't move." Curtis raised the shotgun.

Curtis' father had said the same thing yesterday, "Son, I said don't move."

"It's just an oil filter," he said.

"Well then, it shouldn't be hard to hold that hose back."

"It's just a filter is my point. It can wait." The front end moved with the force his father put on the jammed filter. The metal of the truck felt cold on their hands.

"No it ain't and no it can't. A man's got obligations." He said it all the time. He didn't just say it to his son but the entire police force.

"Ain't the end of the world," Curtis said.

"Don't take a tone."

"Just leave it alone. So I forgot. I'll see to it when I get home."

"You say that. Tomorrow will come and nothing will have changed." His father was a big man. He had hands the size of breakfast plates. "Walk in here, in my station, smelling like beer, smelling like you do every morning."

"Maybe I ain't much different than they are, then," Curtis said.

"There's a right way to do things. I don't aim to bide my time and watch you get all soft, get all native. This ain't a horse son. It ain't going to take care of itself."

"A horse don't take care of itself."

"That isn't the point. You don't forget son. You're a man. You can't forget. You force yourself not to forget because you remember where you come from and you do that shit because you are a man." His father's face was red. He stood out from under the hood and rolled his shoulders back.

"It's just a fucking oil filter."

That's when his father backhanded him. "I said, it ain't the oil filter I'm worried about." The blow split his cheek in two places. The inside skin welted from his molars and his chapped bottom lip cracked from his father's knuckles. He tasted the metal of blood.

After the backhand, Curtis slammed the hood down and left his father wiping his fingers with a red rag. He picked up a case of Schlitz from Larry's Service Station. He was a sixer in by the time he parked in front of his trailer. The trailer, like everything, sat surrounded by the nothing of desert rocks and shrubs. They scattered in every direction. A wooden fence marked the small lot. He dragged blankets to the cheap kitchen chairs and table in the yard, and he sat there in the darkening when Alma Lamont came up the rise to the fence and crawled through it to the yard. The tiny plateau the trailer stood on dropped off into cuts and ditches that fed the creek beds at the bottom during storms.

"Who hit you?"

"Nobody."

"Why you holding that can to your face?" she asked.

"Why you here?"

"Sam dropped me off this morning. I cleaned your trailer up a bit while I waited for you. You ever broom that floor?" Alma pointed with her chin past him to the dented trailer. "I walked down before the sun quit. That river bed's filling up."

Curtis threw the empty beer can. The can arched high and flew through the air slowed like an off speed pitch. Air caught in the summersault of the spin and whistled before the can nicked a fence post and bounced back into the yard.

"What happened to your lip?" Alma picked up the can and added it to the pile scattered around his chair.

"Nothing."

"Something at work today?" she asked.

"I said nothing."

"You're drinking."

"No shit," Curtis pulled open the tab of another beer, "forget it."

Alma crossed her arms and shivered. "Your father phoned. He hung up on me."

"Why did you pick up?" Curtis said. He hooked one of her belt loops with his finger and pulled her toward him.

"Thought it might be you." Alma brushed his hand away and pulled a blanket from his shoulder.

Curtis felt his lip with the hand she swatted. "Goddamn it. I've told you."

"He wasn't very happy."

"Why would I call my own trailer?"

"You remember how mad my father got at senior prom?"

"I'm not talking about you." The cold night wrapped around them. Alma sat down across from Curtis and pulled the blanket to her chin. They were quiet. The wind picked up the ends of Alma's hair and played with it and pushed it into her face. Clouds robbed them of moon light and the usual silhouettes it made.

"They think the siege is going to come to an end soon?"

"Nope."

"Sam's taking me to Albuquerque this weekend."

"It's time to give all that up. Wounded Knee is government land anyway."

"Ma says . . ."

"Screw your mother."

"Curtis." Alma tucked her hair behind her ears.

"Leave it alone. Leave that Wounded Knee shit up there in the Dakotas. We got you and me to deal with."

"Sam agrees, you know?"

"I don't care what Sam thinks. I'm not Marlon Brando. I don't believe in all this shit. Leave it alone."

"Sam says the mayor is a false person. That the border liquor stores are traps. Sam is going to petition." Alma said. She leaned forward on the wobbly chair.

The border towns sold alcohol along the edges of the reservations. Drunks, gloníís, wobbled back in the dark, followed the center line of a highway before it turned into gravel roads. Every year drunks were hit and killed at night, all along the borders. The mayor dealt with more and more heat because while he claimed to fight alcoholism on the reservations he owned most of the liquor stores along the borders.

"Alma, I'm tired of hearing about your mother. I'm tired of hearing about your brother. I'm tired of the goons and the clubs. I am tired of answering these questions all fucking day long and dealing with the same shit when I get home."

"Curtis. You're a part of it, too," Alma said.

"Well, not really. I don't think I care about the Navajo nation or about Wounded Knee. They'll run out of food up there or the government will send in more troops or some shit, but it ain't going to change anything. People are just going to get killed. "

"Curtis, there's a right way to do things."

"Look, Alma, it's nobody's fault that people are drunks either. It's just a shitty world. Them Indians need to pass out and quit walking the roads in the middle of the night."

"Your father thinks it is a problem."

"Alma!" Curtis yelled. He threw the half empty can of beer at her. It missed and landed over the drop against some rocks. The can skidded in the dark. "Alma, quit it. I mean it."

"You mean it?" Alma stood, "Drive me home." Her hair moved in the wind. The sound of open desert whirled around them. It was the sound of friction. It banged the loose door on the trailer. Her blanket fell onto the ground.

"I ain't driving anywhere." Curtis looked at the blanket. The wind drove over their heads. It sounded like the interstate with the windows down. "It's cold. Let's go in." He hooked her belt loop again.

"I'll call Sam then." She turned to the trailer.

Curtis grabbed her wrist.

"Let go."

"You're going to stay."

"I don't think so, Curtis." Alma twisted her wrist in his grip. His hand clamped around her slender arm.

"What do you mean, you don't think so?"

"What do you think I'm talking about? Let go. I'm calling Sam." Alma pulled away from Curtis.

"I said stay here." He jerked her hard by the wrist. Alma fell forward and stumbled and used her free hand to keep from falling to her knees.

"Get off of me."

He dragged her toward the trailer and pushed her up on the wall next to the open door. "You want to know what I think?"

"Get off."

Her back thudded into the wall. He pinned her there with his hand on her chest. "You wanna know what I think!" Curtis yelled. He coughed and cleared his throat.

"Get off me."

With his other hand, he pulled open the front of her pants and then pulled them down. He yanked at them and then used his cold boot to push the jeans down past her knees.

"Get off of me."

"Shut up," Curtis said. He stopped and ran his fingertips along Alma's cheekbone.

"Stop it. Get off. I don't want this."

"I said shut your mouth." He coughed again. Curtis covered her face with his other hand.

She pressed her back against the wall and turned her head. His hand squeezed tight around her mouth and pressed up on her nose. It was hard for her to breathe and her skin burned on the cold wall. The ply board scratched.

He pinned her to the wall and Alma sucked air and pulled up on her jeans. Curtis moved her legs apart with his feet. He spit on his fingers, and reached down between her legs and with his hand on her mouth. He pushed hard. Her hair caught in the fibers of the ply board.

Alma's head and shoulders shook. He uncovered her mouth and took his weight off of her and leaned onto the wall. Alma sniffed and wiped at the snot dripping off her nose. His shoulders dropped, and he moved his body back just enough for Alma to push him away.

"Get away from me, Curtis," she said. The wind kept pushing in over the high mesa. "Just get away from me."

"Alma. Shit. I'm sorry." His boots squeaked on the linoleum.

"That's right. You are sorry." She slapped at him. "You are no different." Alma pushed at the hand still on her chest and pushed Curtis away from her. "There isn't anything to say. It doesn't matter now. You never wanted to, but you've done it."

"What's that?"

"You're a good for nothing drunk."

"Well that just makes me part Indian, don't it?" His eyes got smaller.

"And you are your father." Alma tried to push away from Curtis.

Curtis punched her. He pushed her hard against the wall and held her there at arm's length and he punched her. His fist knocked her head into the wall. Alma looked down at the clean floor. Her hair covered her face. She breathed in hard, filling her lungs.

Staring at the floor she said, "Bilagáana asshole," then she hissed it, "You asshole."

"Don't you dare tell your brother about this," Curtis whispered. He leaned his weight on her again. He covered her mouth and nose. She breathed in gasps. He was rough with her then. He was rough to the end and the sound of the trailer door banged into the frame as the wind pushed against it over and over. His voice stayed low and nonverbal. His voice sounded like the wild boar her father found when she was a girl. The boar grunted and pushed its tan snout into the sandy places. The long, flexible snout crawled through leaves and dirt like a hand looking for something in the dark. Unlike their sheep that yearned for tending, it refused care.

"That animal is out of place," her father said. "It should have stayed in Texas." That year, over half of their lambs died. It disappeared in the hot of summer and her father brought a jaw with tusks home at the beginning of winter. The dry skin of the snout was no longer soft but weathered and papery and it curled in strips.

"It must of fell into a crack and got wedged," her father said.

The jaw sat on the rock pile all winter. In the spring, she touched the dry paper bag skin where she imagined the lip to be. It was tough then. It was something else. The dark places now forever closed off from it.

Alma touched her lip. The wet of tears and blood smeared her fingertips.

Curtis touched the side of her neck with a fingertip.

"That's the last time you touch me," Alma spit out blood onto the floor. "Sam is going to kill you."

"Don't you tell him anything," Curtis let go of her and turned his back to the wall and slid down until he was sitting on the floor. "Don't you say a word."

"Or what," hissed Alma, "you going to rape me again?"

Curtis saw the white of her eyes. "We'll see," Curtis said, "we'll see." He closed his eyes and leaned his head back onto the wall.

She kicked his feet away from her and stepped over his legs. With her pants bunched around her knees, Alma tripped down the trailer steps into the dark and cold. She hopped, stumbled, getting more and more shackled in the twist of clothes around her legs. She made it to the gate post at the beginning of the drive. She peed at the fencepost. Her fingers trembled on the rough wood as she squatted. The twist of jeans and underwear refused to unravel. Alma sat all the way down in the splattered dirt and kicked off her pants. She pulled her knee up with one leg and stretched her other leg out, but the pants strangled around her feet. Her fingers struggled to untie her shoes. She stepped out of the wad of clothing, the gravel road sharp on her feet. Alma wiped the inside of her thighs with her underwear and stuck them on a nail hanging from the gate. She stepped into her pants and her shoes and turned toward the main road. The trailer door tapped into its frame and sounded into the night. The tapping kept off beat with the crunch of her footsteps. The road was dark. The wind pushed at her back messing her hair into a tangle at her face. She pulled it together and stuffed it under her collar.

Sam gripped the steering wheel. He drove leaned forward and his chest almost touched the fake leather stripping around the wheel.

"We are turning around," he said.

"Sam, no. Take me home. I need to go home."

"Alma, I don't care if his father is the chief of police. I don't care that he is Bilagáana asshole. I care about you. What he's done." Sam punched the steering wheel, "What he's done," he said again.

"Just take me home." Alma felt the cool glass of the truck window on her forehead.

"What happened?" The dried plastic grip wrap of the steering wheel creaked under his fingers. He breathed hard. His body tightened. Up and down the pump of his heart beat until the specter of adrenaline withdrew its clawed hand and released his lungs from their cage and the pounding slowed and he breathed.

"How long has this been going on?"

"This?" Alma asked. The pitch of her voice rose. She shifted in the front and her hands braced the seat under her thighs. "This?"

The truck tires rumbled on potholes. He did not see the man in the road until they drove over him. It was the crunch of his fender and his sister's scream he noticed more. She braced her arms. One hand splayed on the passenger side window and the other dug into his arm. The passenger side bumped up and back down and Sam slid the truck to a stop. A flail of limbs flashed past his rear view and was unmistakable and he waited, truck diagonal, on the empty space of road. Alma's eyes were large.

The shape behind him, tinted red from brake lights, lay still. Sam pulled the truck out of gear and took his foot off the brake. The body vanished into the dark and he leaned onto the steering wheel and looked up the road into the weak yellow of his headlights. Gloníís wandered the roads with brown paper bags wrapped around their malt liquors in their hands. They wandered the roads late at night here on the borders, but, unlike the deer that also wandered these empty spaces, they were too drunk to have the sense to leap out of the way.

"Let's roll him into the ditch." Sam nudged an arm with his boot.

"Sam. We can't do that," Alma said. She pressed her hands to the side of her face. The air was cold, but her face felt hot. "What if he's still alive?"

"Alma, what are we going to do?" Sam closed his eyes. "He won't be alive by the time we get anywhere."

"I don't think he's breathing, Sam."

Sam dragged the body to the truck. She hopped onto the bed and pulled.

"Somebody needs to do something about all of this, Alma. We aren't living as much as we're dying."

The only light on the road was the yellow of the headlights.

They closed the tailgate and drove following the dim cones of the truck's headlights. The sound of gravel under the tires and the air whistling at the windows did all the talking for a while.

After a time when neither of them spoke, Sam said, "Kaila's pregnant."

"Oh, Sam," Alma said.

She leaned her head back on the cold glass and closed her eyes. The headlights followed the curves, the unblinking eyes of an owl low on the ground. A shift of the darkness they could not see, a shift of light and wind out toward the mountains began a new day. It happened without notice. The truck followed its headlights into the lifting dark.

With his shotgun raised, Curtis looked for a gun in Sam's hand.

Sam turned. His body kept pivoting. The rock salt continued to crunch under his feet.

"Don't fucking move."

Sam turned all the way around and faced Curtis. His hand hidden by his body for a moment flashed into view.

The bang of the shotgun shattered the quiet of the day in every direction, and Curtis watched the cigarette hang in the air.

"He dropped his cigarette," said his partner. The little bit of blood at their feet began to smear with their boot prints. The white of the cigarette stood out bright on the pavement.

"He didn't have a gun."

"I got him good," said Curtis.

"You had your shotgun up faster than a jack rabbit, dropped him like a jack rabbit."

"He should have stayed holed like a jack rabbit," said Curtis.

"He didn't have a gun."

"It was a cigarette," said Curtis, "He was holding a cigarette."

"Did you know that?"

"I don't know. I think so. Maybe," said Curtis.

"Damn it."

"The mayor's over here," a voice yelled from around the building. Curtis leaned the butt of his shotgun on his hip.

"Mayor okay," asked Curtis.

"He is. What happened?"

"Fucking Indians. What the fuck was he thinking?"

"What are you talking about? You didn't have to shoot him."

"You know who that is, don't you?" Curtis said. The black hair pushed around the head on the pavement and covered the face. Blood didn't pour out onto the sidewalk. There were spots of red here and there and the hair clumped in sticky twists, but it was cold and the blood seemed to stay sopped up by the flannel shirt. A big red patch spread across the chest.

"That's Sam Lamont."

"No shit."

"No shit."

"Fuck. You're right." The men were quiet. "Why did you shoot him? I'll say I shot him. He was going for a gun, right. He was going for a gun. He needs a gun."

"It doesn't matter now," Curtis said, "Why do you care? Alma was never going to forgive me anyway."

The shop window mirrored the young man at their feet. Dead on the pavement, his body reflected around the large green lettering: Guns & Ammo. The two patrol men stood with their backs to the shop. Curtis held his 12 gauge in his right hand. His trigger finger pressed against the trigger guard to steady the weapon. With the butt on the front of his hip, he stayed rocked back a bit so the weapon angled from him and pointed to the sky.

Alma's brother dead at his feet, Curtis tongued a welt on the inside of his lip. He tongued his cheek. He thought about his morning ride into work and his morning woody. He put his hand in his pocket. The bump of the dirt road wouldn't let it go away. The bumping had rubbed it on his leg, and it pushed it against his pants and his pants kept it all balled up until it pushed into a pocket lining like that wad of chaw settling at the bottom of a lip. Curtis sat in the truck for a few minutes before going into Larry's to buy beer.

That first day of March was cold and dirty. Browned snow packed against the edges of the curb running along the downtown street. A thin line of blood dripped off of the curb into the brown slick of oil and ran off with the melt. The blood continued to trickle into the wet and the brown slush caved into a puddle and drifted down the street.

His father walked up the sidewalk. His right hand rested on his firearm. Curtis turned and watched the sunlight as it slipped through a break in the cloud cover, and the clouds in the distance turned darker in the contrast. The puddles on the street sparkled for a moment before cloud cover dimmed their light again. The street ran east west. It ran parallel to the interstate. I-40 disappeared into the world in both directions.

The Tale of Cindy Jack's Mother

The brown sparrow left the pine and dropped out of the wind. Drought-bent grasses pressed close to the shrub bush. The sparrow shook its feathers between short bursts of flight, stopping on a fence wire then another shrub. The little brown bird escaped late summer heat in the direction of the beat-up trailer. Aluminum sides, dulled white by age, settle into the cracked, block foundation. The sparrow skipped along the edge in the dirt and up through a crack under a covered window and disappeared into the dark.

The room above the cracked foundation smelled of forgotten laundry. A large mattress crowded the floor space. Gaps between the mattress and the walls are stuffed with clothing on one side and empty two-liter plastic bottles on the other. Breathing. Deep breathing in the dark gave life to the heavy room. Staggered draws of breath end and hang silent, an unanswered question, then release, a flood of throaty air. So the breathing burdened the room. Edges of mattress slope inward, into the cup of a great hollow. The beast on the mattress turns, and a quick breathing lifts and drops the bent springs. The breathing drowns to the grind of spinning tires from the steep gravel drive.

A rusted truck rattled across the yard to a stop. The driver, a thin man, put the truck in gear and chocked the tire with a wedge of firewood from the bed.

"Come here," he said. He lifted his two daughters from the back. Their hair swirled and knotted, the weave of a bird's nest.

Grocery bags in hand, the three walked through the wind to the front door. Summer sun cooked the insides of the trailer, and the girls always stood at the door and waited, preferring the warm breeze outside to the stagnant heat inside.

Dishes and bottles, spoons glued into old food, covered the counter by the sink. Yellow furniture stuffing clumped on the floor. Empty grocery bags piled in the corner.

Their father scooted a bag of Coca-Cola across the linoleum. One of the bottles thudded over and a crown of white foamed inside the plastic. "Here, take this to her." He set a box of Kentucky Fried Chicken on the floor. "And this."

"I don't want to," said the oldest girl.

"Cindy, watch your attitude." He reached for her shoulder, but the girls stepped back into the doorway. The light of the day pushed their shadows into the trailer.

"I don't like it in there."

"It's not up for debate."

"She smells bad."

"Then you take that," their father said. He pointed his chin to a blue bucket with a washcloth gripping its rim.

"And you," he said, "feed her." He tapped his index finger on the forehead of the youngest girl and then pulled on her long hair letting it slip along his finger.

The girls held hands and leaned against each other.

He smiled and said, "Now."

Cindy carried the wash bucket with both hands. She bent her little legs around the swinging thing as she walked. The sisters' slender bodies slipped into the gap of the bedroom doorway. The door wedged from the inside. The girls struggled in the darkness. Tacked into soft ply board, a faded floral sheet hung over the window. Faint light filtered into the room. It took a moment for their eyes to adjust, so the girls stood at the edge of the mattress breathing through their mouths.

The beast turned. A white sheet, browned, covered the body.

"Give me something to drink."

Cindy twisted the top and a hiss escaped from the bottle of Coca-Cola. After reaching the soft drink across the bed, Cindy pushed the box of chicken along the bedspread. A trail of grease smeared the sheets.

"Don't just stand there," said the beast, "Empty that shit bucket, girl."

In the yard the father turned a wheelbarrow upright. He shoveled sand and stucco and poured water from a hose. Tiny clouds of gray cement floated with every turn of the shovel. The father coughed and pulled the wet through the dry mix until it was sticky mud. Drops of water dotted the dirt and gravel.

The metal trowel scratched across the block wall under the window. The blocks pushed into the dirt and corners crumbled. The trowel's flat side pulled the mud across the block face. Cement filled the cracks and veneered the surface covering everything up.

He watched Cindy empty one of the buckets. After turning it upside down she tapped it on the flat rock he put next to the ditch they dug that summer. Last summer the ditch had been on the other side of the trailer. Her long hair hung around her face. She banged the bucket on the rock. The wind played with the hem of her t-shirt and pushed it up her back. The line of her spine twisted with every bang of the bucket. Then she scooped dirt from the pile next to the ditch and sprinkled it into the hole.

The plate leaned even when he set it on the very edge of the mattress.

"What else?" He asked. He wrinkled his nose and held the back of his hand over his mouth.

"I see the way you look at them."

"They are getting older," he said.

"That's not what I mean. It's the same way you used to look at me."

"It's true," he said. The pile of empty bottles shifted when he pushed at the bottom of pile with the side of his foot.

"You did this to me."

"I like the way you are."

"You mean you like this." She grabbed the flesh of her thigh and flopped it, back and forth, like the rubber shower mat unstuck and rolled over in the tub.

"Don't know."

"It turned you on."

"I don't know," he said. He spoke through the fingers of his hand covering his nose.

"You looked at me, like you were hungry."

"You were always hungry. You wanted me to feed you."

"Don't kid yourself," her hoarse laughter shook the bed. "You got off on keeping me here. Keeping me fed."

"It's not the same," he said.

"I won't let you do this to them," she said. She grabbed the fat of her leg again and jiggled it.

"You haven't left this room in three years," he said.

"You're mine. This is what you like." She pushed the sheet down.

"The foundation is falling apart," he said. "I'll probably work on it after I take them to school tomorrow." The room grew dark quickly when the sun dropped behind the mountains along the horizon. He squinted in the dim light. "Anything else," he said again.

Only a belabored breathing answered him. He doubted she fell asleep, but he left without another word anyway, pulling the door behind him until the latch clicked.

Morning sun strayed along the outside of the trailer. The girls stood at the bedroom door. The beast never ate breakfast.

"Say bye to your mother," their father said. He walked out to start the truck.

Some mornings they stood there toeing the edge of the mattress, hoping not to be called over for a hug or a kiss. The breath stank. They hurriedly talked about chores and math problems, so they wouldn't have to get too close.

"She was mean yesterday," Alivia, the youngest of the two girls, said. The girl looked down at the floor while she spoke.

"Just to me. She likes you," said Cindy.

"I don't like it when she's mean to you. She should use the bathroom like we do."

Cindy squeezed her sister's hand. "Come on."

This morning the bedroom stayed closed and the snoring followed them into the yard.

"Let's go," yelled their father. He slapped the metal side of his door with the palm of his hand. They never spoke on the way to school. The radio was broken, and the girls shared the passenger seat belt so they could crowd together on the far side of the front seat.

The bus had already pulled into the parking lot of the Come-N-Go gas station.

"Chicken Noodle's grandmother bringing you home?" Their father asked, referring to Cindy's best friend. That old woman, an old Navajo woman, didn't like him very much.

"Yes."

"Yes?"

"Yes, sir, we'll ride home with her this afternoon."

"Better hurry before it leaves. I ain't driving you into town."

He stood there looking at the cinder blocks. The foundation on the back side of the trailer shifted. The sun, still rising, left the back side in shadow. The hose in his hand filled the wheelbarrow. The peaks of orange sand sank below the rising surface. Water crested the rim and splashed into the dirt and on his boots.

"Shit."

"What is it?" she said from inside the room.

"Don't worry about it," he yelled at the wall. He kicked the wheelbarrow over and the masonry mix sloshed into the ditch.

The propane line ran up into the trailer at the corner. The black rubber line slipped through a hole he busted into the block years ago. He always meant to patch this back side. He turned off the water and left the wheelbarrow on its side, draining its dirty lake.

Stuffing loose clothes and sheets under the girl's bedroom door and pulling long stretches of duct tape reminded him of the brown birds around the trailer. Every year they rebuilt their nests. His fingers trembled. Ash from his cigarette fell to the floor.

"I want one of those," said the voice from the room.

"I'll bring you my pack before I pick up the girls from school," he said.

His fingers tapped the stuffing into small cracks around the doors and windows. Around the room he pushed socks and small t-shirts into the gaps, and he pressed the silver duct tape along the edges covering everything up, holding everything in.

He unscrewed the propane from the stove. The black hose hissed on the floor. A red brick from outside kept the hose pointing into the main room out from the kitchen.

"Here're cigarettes," he said. He tossed the pack on the bed.

"What's that smell?"

"I had to mess with the propane line."

"Why do I smell it in here?" she asked. She covered her nose and mouth with a puffy hand. Her voice uncertain and questioning became quiet and she coughed.

"It's not that bad," he said, "Maybe I bled the line too much. Don't worry about. It'll be fine."

"Why are you picking them up today?"

"Cindy told me Chicken Noodle's grandmother can't do it. She's in the hospital or something."

"Poor thing," she said.

"Yeah, poor thing," he said, "I'm going to leave your door open until I get back." He slid a rusty garbage can up against the door. It scratched a groove into the linoleum.

"You forgot to bring me my lighter," she yelled.

He turned at the front door. All the cracks were filled. The yellow foam stuffed into the gaps around the door jambs. It should stay airtight.

"I put a book of matches in that pack," he yelled back.

"I think I want chicken again tonight," she yelled back.

"Okay," he said. He let the screen door bang into its frame and walked to the truck.

Down the driveway the gravel crushed under his tires. It might take a few cigarettes before it happened. Hopefully he stuffed up all the cracks. That gas might take a bit to fill the trailer. At the turn in the road he stopped and watched the sun shining onto the glass of her bedroom window.

The girls hated the trailer. They hated how hot it got. They hated the smell. None of that bothered him. What bothered him was the way the trailer shackled him. How she shackled him. He loved how she relied on him for everything in the beginning. When she got so big that she couldn't leave the room, he stopped locking the door. He stopped worrying that she would leave him. Then the girls arrived. Consumed by hunger, she never spent time with their children.

He would pay for his sins. He knew that, but she was wrong about him. The girls needed him. They didn't need her.

He pulled a cigarette from his shirt pocket and pushed in the black knob of the lighter beside the ashtray. The sun continued to reflect off the window and the aluminum frame. When he turned his head, the sun's reflection looked like a spark playing along the side of the trailer.

He eased the truck into gear and continued down the long gravel drive.

After the knob popped, he pulled the glowing eye from the socket and pressed the red coil to the tip of his cigarette. That spark of sunshine ran along the trailer's edge until the trailer disappeared from his rearview mirror. Breathing deep, he steadied himself so that the cigarette between his fingers stopped trembling. He took one last drag and flicked the butt out the window into the dry grasses clumped along the ditch beside the road.

The Secret of Old Man Gloom

Cindy tried hard to hide it. He knew though. He even understood. Hiding a feeling was like covering a fire pit with a newspaper. It took no time at all before tongues and flames danced around the edges and gobbled the entire thing up. Feelings were one thing though. Chicken Noodle knew Cindy was hiding more than feelings. It was the way she wore a hoodie in summer or tugged on the cuffs of her sleeves to make sure they were still doing their jobs, covering up something underneath, something she didn't want anybody, even him, to see.

"What are you looking at," Cindy asked when he spotted the wedged lighter.

"Nothing."

"Keep it that way," Cindy said.

Chicken Noodle fished the round side of the blue lighter stuck between the seats with a finger. The back of his hand grazed Cindy's, and she pulled her hand back.

"What are you doing?"

"Saw this lighter," he said. He flicked it, but it only sparked.

"Good for you," said Cindy.

Chicken Noodle pressed his forehead to the passenger window of the pickup truck. He turned when he felt her fingers brush against his leg. Her finger nail picked a seam on the seat.

When did she start painting her nails pink? The seam ran half under his thigh, and her knuckles rubbed against his jeans as Cindy kept pulling the end of a thread.

A skinny bug struggled along the rubber weather strip of the inner truck window. Its fan blade wings flickered then settled along its body. The bug shimmered its wings again. It buzzed them so the remaining daylight pulled along their edges in an iridescent line. Its feet tickled Chicken Noodle's skin as it crawled across his wrist into the cup of his hand.

Driving to Santa Fe for the burning of Zozobra was his Grandfather's idea, but it was okay when Cindy said she wanted to come along.

"A waste of time," is all Grandmother said. Cindy rolled her eyes at Chicken Noodle and even smiled. "You stay with me." Grandmother pulled Cindy's sister close.

After the trailer fire, the girls moved into Chicken Noodle's room. He slept on a pile of blankets in Grandfather's room. Every night Grandfather shifted under the sleepless watch of darkness. Was Cindy asleep?

"George," Raul said. "It'll just be a few days, until I can figure out a living situation." The girls stood so close together they looked two-headed. Last summer, a lamb was born with two heads. It didn't live long. Grandmother tsked when she saw it.

Raul put his hand on Cindy's shoulder. She leaned away and her hair fell back off her shoulder when she shifted her weight.

"We don't have much room," said Grandfather.

"But, Grandfather," said Chicken Noodle.

"Of course they will stay here," interrupted his Grandmother. She stood in the doorway behind them. She stepped off the stoop and pushed the girls out of the bright sun back into the shadow of the doorway. She stared at her husband for a moment and then turned to Raul. "They will stay here as long as they need," she said.

Those few days turned into weeks, and now the first month of school was over and Cindy's father still worked on rebuilding the blown up trailer.

On the weekends, Chicken Noodle and Grandfather helped lay the new block foundation. The first few times, they raked soot-covered block and melted plastic out of the clearing. Was it true what other kids said? Was Cindy's mother a monster—crawled back into the canyons? After the trailer fire, Cindy didn't talk about her mother. She never wanted to come to help clean up.

"Zozobra is bigger than a tree," Grandfather said in the truck.

The stunted pines on the side of the road were just taller than the cab of their passing pickup. "He is filled with gloom, and when he burns our problems burn away."

"Sounds lame," said Cindy, "way too easy."

"Sometimes things are easy."

"Things are never easy," said Cindy.

When they arrived the marionette hulked across from them, across the field of people, a giant ogre surveying the ranks before battle. Burning him destroyed the worries and troubles of the previous year. It all burned up in the flames, Chicken Noodle's grandfather insisted. Anyone who wanted to get rid of worries from the past year drove by the offices of the *Santa Fe Reporter* in the weeks leading up to the burn to drop off slips of paper with personal gloom written on them. The papers then dumped into a gloom box were placed at Zozobra's feet to be burned.

"I wish we could have dropped off our own papers," said Cindy.

"Maybe if we lived closer," said Grandfather.

"We don't live close to anything," said Cindy.

"You two wait here," said Grandfather.

"We always have to wait," Chicken Noodle said to Cindy. With his fist by his ear, he felt the trapped bug blur its wings. "Want to see what I caught?"

Cindy covered a paper on her knee, shielding it with her hand, like a math test. "Where's he going?" she said.

"I don't know," Chicken Noodle said. He held his trapped bug at Cindy's ear. "What are you writing?"

"Nothing. Leave me alone." Cindy turned on the seat and Chicken Noodle stuck his tongue out at her back.

"Look at everybody," Cindy said when they parked. The crowd

spread out from the parking lot everywhere. The sunset purpled the sky. She opened the glove box and asked Grandfather if she could have a faded mechanic receipt.

"That's fine, but don't go wandering off," he said, after telling them to wait by the truck.

Now he squeezed Chicken Noodle's shoulder and kept repeating the same words. "Damn it."

The fry bread Grandfather brought back sat on the hood of the car. It smelled sweeter than Grandmother's. The white sugar disappeared into the warmth of the bread.

No sooner did Grandfather say not to wander off, and Cindy wandered off.

"Damn it." Grandfather put both hands on Chicken Noodle's shoulders, grounding him from leaving like the metal frame holding up Zozobra. "Why did you let her go?"

It wasn't like it was Chicken Noodle's fault. He almost lost his bug. It crawled through a gap by his thumb and hopped to the warm metal of the truck. Chicken Noodle snatched at it.

"Did you see that?" Chicken Noodle said, but when he turned Cindy was gone.

Chicken Noodle and Grandfather pushed through the crowd looking for Cindy.

"Have you seen a little girl? This tall?" Grandfather asked everyone and held the flat of his hand over Chicken Noodle's head.

Before the head of the marionette caught fire, the crowd moved in crazy rhythm. The groaning voice from the speaker chanted. Everybody pumped fists in the air and screamed and the groaning voice of Zozobra grew bigger and bigger while the swaying, moving crowd cheered louder and louder.

"Damn it," Grandfather said again.

"What if we don't find her?" Chicken Noodle closed his fingers into a hollow fist. He could feel the bug tickle around the gaps by his thumb.

"Give me your hand," Grandfather said. He grabbed Chicken Noodle's balled up hand and moved back toward the truck. "Maybe we'll see her from up on the hill."

Chicken Noodle walked fast and tried to keep his fist hollow. He tried to feel if the bug was still moving around, but Grandfather jerked him up the hill.

"Maybe she's back at the truck."

They didn't see her. Grandfather grabbed men by their shoulders and pushed them back looking in and out, between every clump of people.

"What the fuck, dude," said a slow-talking kid. He wore a woolly toboggan.

Grandfather stepped back and forth between groups of people, an elaborate dance.

"You're hurting my hand." Chicken Noodle ran to keep up, dragged along by Grandfather's strong grip. He couldn't feel the bug flicking around in the cave of his fist. He couldn't feel it at all. It was crushed.

More and more people left their parked cars and trucks as the fire grew and the moaning reverberated out of the loud speakers. The late comers were like the flies stuck to the sticky tape on Grandmother's windows. The lines of people slowed as they bunched up, as if their feet were sticking to the ground.

Across the park, far above the crowd's many heads, burned the large puppet, Zozobra. It was ten times taller than Grandfather described. It disappeared into the sky. Its arms stretched out wide and the unburned face grinned. The grin reminded him how Cindy smiled when she stole money from her dad's wallet. Her eyes almost glowed with glee, and she put a finger to her lips, binding him to keep her secret.

Grandfather let go of his hand. Chicken Noodle opened a couple fingers and there it was—the long legged bug fidgeted and buzzed its wings on its back. He tried to cover his open hand with his other hand, but the bug jumped and flew away before he could catch it.

"Go find Cindy," Chicken Noodle called after the little flyer.

They walked back down into the crowd of people, and the fire began to burn high on the robes. The light from the burning man pushed out around everybody.

They were deep in the crowd. Everyone packed together.

"Look, Grandfather," Chicken Noodle said. He pointed to a gap of the crowd and there Cindy walked, this way and that, looking up at the faces of the adults around her. Her own face streaked with tears. Her bangs stuck to her head. She ran toward them when she saw them.

"Cindy," Grandfather said. He pushed a man out of his way. "We have been looking for you." Grandfather kneeled on the ground. Everywhere people cheered and the speakers groaned and the orange light of the fire flickered shadows across all the faces.

"I'm sorry." Cindy stopped and stood with her head down.

"Where have you been?"

"I wanted to burn this," she said. She held out a folded square of paper receipt from the truck. "I wanted to burn something too."

"I told you to stay close."

"I know."

"Come here." Grandfather hugged her. Cindy held her shoulders up, with her hands by her side.

"I needed to burn it," Cindy cried. "I needed to burn it." She leaned into Grandfather's arms and cried.

"I know," he said again.

Grandfather let go of Cindy, and Chicken Noodle stepped up and hugged her. He squeezed her tight. He could feel her shiver. She didn't hug him back. "I'm glad you're okay, Cindy," he whispered in her ear.

The flames from the burning marionette circled the head and the frantic moaning repeated over and over as the head and arms swung back and forth pulling rolling fire through the air like a fire dancer. The skeleton of Zozobra stuck through burned off sections of robe and the iron frame of the skull outlined by bright fire blackened. An eye socket burned empty. With a final shudder, the loud moan ended and the marionette hung limp and the left over fire consumed the remains. Fireworks launched into the dark and cracked over the frenzy and cheering of the crowd.

A set of fireworks exploded from the mouth of the burned puppet and then on their side of the field, and it made Chicken Noodle's grandfather jump. The crowd continued to yell. People stuck their fists in the air and howled. When the fireworks stopped, the fire's light dimmed. The smoldering skeleton hung limp and defeated. The faces of people all around them drifted back into darkness.

"Let's go," said Grandfather. "We might as well leave now—beat everybody out of the parking lot."

In the cab of the truck, a quiet surrounded them. It was interrupted once in a while with a left over shudder from Cindy's crying. The road darkened when the lights of Santa Fe disappeared behind them. Cindy put her hand on the top of Chicken Noodle's hand. Her skin, smooth, not tickly like bug's feet. She curled her fingers between his fingers and they sat so close their legs pushed against each other through the curve of the road. After a while, her head leaned on his shoulder, and she stopped crying.

The drive home lasted forever. Grandfather almost carried Cindy to the house. She shuffled her feet like a zombie. "Come on, you two," said Grandfather.

"What's wrong with the girl?" he heard his grandmother whisper.

"She's worn out," said Grandfather. Chicken Noodle didn't hear what else Grandfather said.

"Noodle, let's go," said Grandmother. Then, she too, disappeared into the house.

Chicken Noodle stayed sitting. Lights turned on and turned off from one room to another. Every time the darkness around the house pushed away. It was like the darkness was learning to swim and pushing away from the bank of a swimming hole when the lights came on only to fight quickly back to shore as the lights for each room turned back off. Cindy's crumpled square of paper had fallen to the floorboards. He twisted it in his fingers, but he didn't open it.

Past the garden, behind the shed, Chicken Noodle kneeled down. The cold of the earth crept through his jeans around his knees. Darkness. The moon already dipped down below the mountains, and the sun still slept. Everything slept.

Chicken Noodle rubbed the folded paper with his thumbs. The fibers rolled up like boogers. The paper thinned. He lifted an edge of the fold for a moment but closed it before opening up her secret. The lighter from the truck! He pulled it from his pocket and rolled the flint. It sparked. It created a mini firework, a burst of energy pushing back the dark. He flicked it again. It sparked again.

"Come on, stupid thing."

This time a tiny blue flame hovered above the metal mouth of the lighter. Chicken Noodle held the corner of the paper closer and closer to the flame. He held his breath. He held as still as possible, but the paper shivered between his fingers. The flame trembled and grew smaller, a tiny blue dot. Then the corner of the paper wicked yellow and one finger of flame lifted from the paper. Chicken Noodle turned the paper so the flame ran up the side. For a moment the light pushed around Chicken Noodle and the rocks and grasses. The little bushes at the end of the clearing pushed their necks out of the darkness.

"Grandmother says it's time to come in," said Cindy.

Her voice surprised him. He let the lighter slip from his fingers.

There she stood at the edge of the yard. Tears ran down her cheeks and dripped from her chin.

"I didn't know you were there," said Chicken Noodle.

Cindy shrugged. Even though she was crying she smiled. She said thank you so quietly he couldn't hear it, he could just see it, and the paper burned out, and the darkness pushed back around them. Cindy grabbed his hand. She curled her fingers with his. They walked toward the bright glow of lights peeking out from windows and from around the frame of the door that Cindy must have left cracked open when she came out to find him.

It will all burn up in flames. That's what his Grandfather said. The lighter lay forgotten on the ground but Chicken Noodle didn't care. He squeezed Cindy's hand before letting go and closing the door behind them.

Trash

It was one of those New Mexico summers digging its heels into the bloodied dirt of October—refusing a new season take its place. Everyone spent weekends outdoors, hoarding the sun, now that the heat was less suffocating.

Above the golf courses public pools reopened, and, after dropping children off for the afternoon, divorced mothers from snob hill, from the Heights, practiced their concealed weapons license, posing next to the shot-up poster of masked gunmen at the end of a round of gunfire. These pictures post to their web pages, to scare off ex-husbands or Mexican gang members or each other.

Girls looking to get jobs at local strip clubs spend extra hours laying out. Truckers appreciate this attention to detail, even if some of the locals don't care to notice.

Gas station attendants take their time with the morning garbage. Black hefty bags dribble a trail across the pavement. Lot rats follow these trails. The kids sift through dumpsters. They drink left-over Coffee Mate creamers thrown away after the morning rush. They lick the small plastic cups clean. Sometimes the curl of a girl's pink tongue catches the eye of a businessman stopping for the day's paper. These men think these girls will do anything. Raul knows they will do anything.

Raul left the house early. After the trailer fire, social services got in the way. He might see Cindy again tonight though.

They shared secrets. That he missed most.

His pickup pulled a short trailer strapped with weed eaters and blowers and yard tools. He earned two hundred dollars a week.

Before blowing the lot, he cleaned with a bucket in one hand and a clawed pick-up tool in the other. Now and again, he reached down to put something in his pocket.

A tall kid shot-gunned a forty. He leaned at the back wall. "I needed that." A plastic bag with two unopened cans leaned at his feet.

"Good for you, fellow," said Raul. It went something like this every Saturday.

After weed whacking the late summer weeds, the girl propositioned him again while he changed out of his cover pants. He pulled them over his shorts, to shield from flying grit. "Mmm, man, I wish I come by here a minute sooner," she said. Her skinny legs long and brown.

"You would have been disappointed."

"I don't think so." She stood straight. "I don't think so," she said again.

"I do."

"For that twenty you found, we could find out."

Raul laced his boots. The girl turned back to the station. He took a sip from a pint and slid it back under the child's seat strapped into the cab.

She had been working up the nerve all summer. Raul lifted his gas-powered blower from the trailer.

The girl reached under the vending machines. She found a few sticky quarters because she returned from the front with a gas station sausage peeking out of the wrapper in one hand, so red nitrate was the first ingredient.

"Watch it," said Raul, "that's going to slip out."

An old white lady at the pump, probably from Augusta Road, held her purse tight.

The girl opened the aluminum wrapper. She pushed the sausage a bit too hard, and it slipped onto the pavement.

"Oh, man," she said.

The kid next to her picked it out of the sand. He held the dog dangling from his fingers.

"No, man," said Raul.

The kid blew off the hot dog and took a bite.

"Here," Raul said, "get another." He pulled out a single from his pocket. The bill shivered at the end of his out stretched fingers.

The young kid licked his fingers. "You bad. With your dollar bill you bad, ain't you?"

Raul held it out until the kid took it.

"Cindy told us what you do. This one dollar ain't going to save you."

"What do I do?"

"Did she get you this outside job, or did you get her that inside job?"

"What job?"

"You cleaning these lots after a week of drunks, and your little girl come in behind you and clean the inside out of drunks."

After blowing the parking lot free of sand and cigarette trash, Raul strapped his blower to the side of the truck.

The girl walked toward the truck. Raul didn't light his cigarette. He shoved his bottle of whisky between his thighs. She shook her head, barely.

At the passenger side window the young kid appeared. "Hey, man."

"What is it?" Raul looked away from the girl.

"You got another dollar?"

"I got nothing."

"I know you got another dollar, man. I seen you pick shit out of that trash."

"Look, kid, I got nothing."

"You don't want to mess with me."

"I ain't interested in you." Raul said.

"She'll be earning at that bathroom tonight. That interests you."

"Who's that?"

"Don't matter. It's always somebody's little girl, ain't it? Either way, you the perv."

Long legs stretched in his rear view. He pulled onto the highway. The metal trailer clattered. A wheel dropped off the curb. An empty glass pint slipped to the floorboards. Raul reached into his pocket and pulled the dirty twenty he found crumpled on the pavement. He lifted it to his nose. It smelled of sweat and gasoline. Down the road sirens cried, answering each other, lamenting. Too late. . . too late. . . too late.

How the Butcher Bird Finds Her Voice

From his knees, Grandfather tied the legs of the sheep together. It kicked out a couple of times. The gray animal stilled, breathing on its side in the dirt. Every time we killed a sheep, Grandfather showed us the same steps.

"Pay attention," he said.

Cindy picked up the large knife Grandfather brought from the kitchen.

"Put that down," Grandfather said.

"It's okay," Grandmother contradicted.

Grandfather frowned. He swept his fingers up and down across the throat of the animal. He picked out goat-heads and burrs. He patted the wool clean.

Cindy lived with us now. Her father was a deadbeat, Grandmother said.

"Shove that closer," Grandfather said. He pointed to the large ceramic bowl at my feet.

I nudged it forward.

"Let her cut," said Grandmother.

Grandfather squinted in the sunlight. "Okay, child, pull the blade across the throat here," he said. His finger drew an unseen line just under the head of the sheep. "The skin will open quickly, but you need to cut deeper and deeper."

Cindy stepped behind grandfather and kneeled onto the sheep, just like Grandfather showed us many times before. He held the bowl with both hands. It fit the shape where the curve of the neck joined the head.

Grandmother smiled. She didn't see me looking at her, but her rare smile signaled things I didn't understand and things I didn't care to understand. Cindy saw the smile, too, and placed the blade at the animal's neck. Grandmother spent more and more time with Cindy, and that was okay to be honest. It meant Cindy spent more and more time with all of us.

"Hold the head," Grandfather said. He curled Cindy's hand around the muzzle of the sheep. The lamb's tongue pulled back between velvety gums, still free of any permanent incisors.

Cindy placed the blade to the throat of the animal again.

"Pull back on the head and pull your blade through."

The first cut opened wide. A red spurt splashed into the white sides of the bowl. The animal's eyes darted. It twitched with surprise. It always surprised me how quiet the taking of life could be. The simple sounds of being, our breathing our movement, drowned out birds and conversation and the other natural sounds of the afternoon.

Cindy pulled the knife across the flayed neck. More life flowed into the bowl. She cut again and again. Blood pumped fast and steady. It filled the bowl. The air smelled heavy, like rain.

Grandfather's hands guided the bowl. He moved it just enough as the sheep tried to kick so as not to spill blood onto the ground.

Cindy cut deeper and deeper. I wasn't sure how the head was still attached or how much more blood could possibly stream from the animal.

From one moment to the next, the struggled ended. It shuddered to an end. Grandfather placed the bowl of blood to the side. Bright red gleamed around the edges, but the deep middle frothed thick and brown. Mud after a storm.

Cindy stood. Her hands stained red from slaughter. A single tear streaked down her cheek. It shone in the sun.

Cindy laughed.

"Good," Grandmother said, "It is good to laugh. When we wash the stomach, we should all giggle and laugh."

I rolled my eyes at Cindy. She giggled some more.

Grandfather showed us how to roll the sheep on its back. He

showed us where to cut the skin around the legs, up the belly. We spent some time, everyone with a knife, skinning, cutting and butchering the animal.

Grandmother put her hand on Cindy's shoulder.

"You, girl, make an old woman proud," she said, "today you found your voice."

Cindy scratched dried, red flakes of blood from her wrists. The birds in the yard called back and forth from secret places. The sun cast down heat. Our faces and our arms and our necks radiated that heat into the glow of the afternoon. I helped grandfather clean up.

Grandmother and Cindy stood in the yard, heads bent toward each other, sharing more secrets, other secrets, ideas of this world or not of this world, ideas full of meaning and wonder, ideas both a part of and devoid of reality. They stood so closely together that their forms and the shadow they cast became indistinguishable. It was hard to tell where one person began and the other ended.

Again Cindy giggled. Her voice carried up, up into the sky and joined those free from the bonds that tie us to the ground. The clear sound of her laughter joined to my heart. Even without a knife, she controlled that deep thumping drum inside my chest.

Cindy Jack and the Town Drunks

Cindy Jack decided early in the school year to kill the town drunks. She and Chicken Noodle were in the backseat of his grandmother's Oldsmobile on the way to school, and as Cindy picked at her finger nail, she made her decision. The vinyl seats smelled sweaty and stuck to her thighs in the heat, and everything about Chicken Noodle's grandmother was creepy.

One time, when they rode home from school Grandmother said, "That would not have been the color of blood anyway." Chicken Noodle had given her a hand drawn card for valentines. It was a big brown heart.

"There wasn't any more red paper," Chicken Noodle replied.

"You make me feel like a million food stamps," she said to Chicken Noodle.

Cindy and Chicken Noodle giggled. Grandmother did not.

The drunks snaked from the parking lot to the bathroom on the side of the gas station. An old man leaned on the dumpster. His hair tangled in the wind. He scratched rust with a rock and kept peeking through the gap of the locked sliding door on the dumpster. A splatter of piss darkened the edge of the dumpster and the pavement. Drunks sat on the curb around the corner. They hunched over their knees, coats sagging to the pavement. The cinder block wall of the station shielded them from the bright gas station lights and the blowing wind. The wire on an unused flag pole clanked against metal. As soon as the drunks ran off, coyotes sniffed at the edges of the concrete pad where the dumpster sat.

The lights turned the garbage around the dumpster into a moon-scape, like the crawl space in January when her dad realized the toilet was flushing into the dirt under the trailer.

"Straight fucking piping," he called it.

He slammed a toolbox on the empty counter top. A wave of beer cans crashed into the wall.

Handing her a flashlight, he said, "Follow me."

The frozen clumps of toilet paper ran like mountain ranges. The tiny peaks circled from the mouth of the broken pipe, waves frozen in place before escaping to a faraway shore. It wasn't just toilet paper puddled in frozen dams. A year's worth of tampons stuck in the sludge. Even with the cold, she breathed through her mouth. The slopes of the mini mountains tugged long shadows from her imagination into dark corners. She lifted the flashlight higher, illuminating the broken pipe.

The nylon string around her father's fingers sawed into the plastic. The sweet smell of a struck match swirled around them.

That night her door banged open.

"It's not your room."

Stale breath settled on her neck. "It's not what you think," he said.

He slumped into her bed.

Her mind joined the shrikes at her grandmother's house. They pulled out the pretty feathers of the goldfinch, leaving their soft bellies open in the air.

The next day, after her father replaced the pipes, she helped him spread the lye. They crawled through that space to cover the mess with ash, a falling snow on the dumpster at the gas station parking lot. She liked it when it snowed. It hid the bare, ugly things on the surface, even if for just a little bit.

Cindy always wore her uniform skirt with a white button up shirt. She pulled her socks up to her knees over stockings. She wasn't really a whore.

"I don't go all the way," she told the girls at school.

"What do you do?" they giggled.

"Just enough," Cindy said.

"Cindy, it's kind of creepy."

"I know," Cindy said.

Their eyes widened with something close to excitement. It was not like a presents on Christmas morning sort of thing but an uncomfortable excitement where imaginations go wild, where imaginations follow shadows into dark places, where things are sticky and wet.

"Does she do it for money?" they whispered, "Why does she do it?"

They shrugged at each other in the mirror, and sucked their teeth, and raised their eyebrows. And Cindy, sitting on the toilet, with her long socks wrinkled and sagged at her ankles, asked for one of the girls preening in front of the mirror to turn on the faucet. Cindy peed and listened to the water splash from the faucet in the sink.

The idea of killing the drunks rooted into her mind one afternoon at Chicken Noodle's house, but it was too much to think about all at one time—so the idea stretched into Cindy's mind over many months—vines circling and weaving and following the light of day around a fencepost.

Some weekends Chicken Noodle's grandfather marched them out into the desert. They followed snakes around. Sometimes they followed a fox Cindy never saw. Some days they listened to Chicken Noodle's grandfather while he pointed out the prickly pear and the pinyon tree. He knew the name of every plant. He pointed to the sagebrush and explained how it and the pinyon tree stayed green all year and that the leaves made a good tea if you were sick. He showed them plants to use if you wanted to get someone sick. The yucca and juniper were good dyes. He collected the pinyon nuts for a snack. The blue green needles of the pinyon tree hovered over its twisted trunk. On days when the sun was too hot and the scattered clouds not enough relief, the three wanderers sat under the shade of a leaning pinyon and waited for the sun's heat to ease.

George remembered stories about the animals and the plants. He told them as truth. Some stories started from the beginning. Cindy loved the ones of transformation. The stories of witches and skinwalkers, those who go on all fours, were told for vengeance.

Cindy shrieked when George dropped to his hands and knees and yipped liked a coyote. He explained to them why it was important to bury their fingernails and hair and to kick dirt over their pee. A skinwalker cursed a person, or even became a person, with the magic of a single clipped finger nail or a strand of hair.

Most days the three of them just hiked the desert in a quiet line. After one of these walks with the rise of the far off southern Rockies dark blue at their backs, they returned home and Grandmother pulled rows through the garden. She stood often with a fist pressed in her side.

At the edge of the yard, Chicken Noodle chased a snake, but it slid off a rock and slipped away. Chicken Noodle and Grandfather were at the rock pile at once. Both of them on their knees moving their hands and pointing to each other. The rocks were big. They scraped against each other when shifted. Chicken Noodle rattled a stick in a gap.

Grandmother lifted her shoulders and rubbed her neck but never turned to look at the rock pile. She leaned on the handle, both hands holding it close to her body. Her eyes closed.

"Grandmother, why do they do that?" Cindy said.

"Because they never grow up."

"But why do they do that?" Cindy said.

She pointed to a shrike on the barbed wire roll leaned against the shed. Its tiny talons perched on the wire, and it pulled at the feathers of a goldfinch with its beak and twisted its head. The songbird impaled to the wire from a barb. The shrike jerked its head back and buried its beak in the belly. A yellow feather stuck to its beak. The gray bird hopped up to the roof and turned its head back and forth, rubbing the feather off on the edge of the asphalt tile.

The old woman leaned on her yard rake. "Because they can. Sometimes it is good to be cruel," said Grandmother, "Sometimes it is all there is. The shrike is slow and weak. It makes up for slow and weak by being the butcher."

Grandmother leaned the rake handle on the rough plaster of the house. She lifted a tiny body from the outside sill of the kitchen window. The lizard was the length of her hand and it stiffened like a rubber toy. The belly skin curled open from a jagged rip between its ribs.

"Why do you keep them on the window?" asked Cindy.

"I can see them there," said Grandmother, "I like to remember."

"But why?" said Cindy.

"I ask myself that too. It is hard letting go of a loved one before you are ready to let go." Grandmother flicked the dried skin of the lizard. "It is hard letting go of the anger."

Cindy touched Grandmother's arm, a light caress with her fingertips.

"Cindy, come on," said Chicken Noodle, "we have it." He pointed at the rattle-snake in his grandfather's hands. The fat belly hung from one arm and the other hand pinched the back of the head. Grandfather and grandson walked away from the garden and the rock pile. They left Cindy and Grandmother standing by the kitchen window.

Chicken Noodle yelled, "Come on, Cindy."

"We shouldn't even touch them," said Grandmother.

"Grandfather said if you watch a snake crawl out of its skin, you will jump out of your own skin."

Grandmother smiled at Cindy and turned Cindy's hand palm up and placed the sun-warmed body of the lizard with its split belly, wobbling, into her hand. "I kill snakes now," she said.

"Doesn't that make Grandfather angry?" asked Cindy.

"All things are alive to be dead, when the time comes," Grandmother said. She pointed at the barbed goldfinch. "When the time comes, death comes. It is never too late. It is never too early."

The lizard weighed nothing in her hand. Cindy pinched its tail.

"What about accidents?"

"Those two will walk out all afternoon and leave that snake in some rocks far from here, but a snake always comes back. When it does, I don't walk with it out into the rocks. I turn it with the end of this handle. I turn it into the soil of my garden." Grandmother twisted a divot into the dirt at their feet, a small dark grave. The shrike, the butcher of birds, whistled twice. A high sinking note challenged another bird pecking at the edge of the garden.

"Some men are like snakes," said Grandmother, "and a snake doesn't know why the butcher bird hunts him, kills him. I don't think the butcher bird always knows. Sometimes she leaves a body to spoil in the sun. I watch all afternoon and she never comes back."

"That doesn't make sense." Cindy packed dirt back into the hole at their feet.

Grandmother pulled earth again. The rake cut, leaving dark lines. "Maybe not, but I kill snakes now. I hold lizards. Despite the old ways, I do these things." The red dirt added the color of blood to Grandmother's eyes when she stopped raking and stared at Cindy. Those eyes swirled the colors of the earth. "The world changes without us," Grandmother said more to herself than to Cindy.

Cindy sniffed at the lizard. All she smelled was the dryness of the day and the flavor of the earth.

"I should have killed them sooner," Grandmother said.

At the edge of the garden, Grandmother picked up an old bowie knife from a woven basket and put it in Cindy's other hand. The knife extended as long as Cindy's arm. Grandmother's eyes were dark brown again. For a moment a shrike whistled, metal shifting on metal, and then a faraway laugh from Chicken Noodle quieted the bird. The air thinned and eased light into the afternoon. Cindy breathed through her nose and closed her eyes. The grooved handle of the knife fit the curl of her fingers.

"Snakes hide and wait and sneak, but only when they are startled do they defend themselves as if their hiding is our fault," Grandmother said, "Don't feel bad."

Cindy didn't know when it started. That's a lie. She knew how it started. If she didn't count that cold night in her bedroom after the

pipe was fixed, nights leading up to it, or the Loggerhead Shrike pulling out the spine of lizards for no reason at all, if those weren't the moments when it actually started, then she did know how it started. It started with a red slushie. At the gas station counter, she pulled the sticky lever from the slushie machine. She wiped the stickiness from her fingers on the edge of the laminate counter. The shrike cleaned her beak back and forth over the roof shingles at Grandmother's garden. After tearing into the body of a finch, the tiniest white belly feathers stayed glued to her beak, so she hopped up to use the edge of the roof.

One of the town gloníís wobbled behind her. He walked up and down the same aisle. Cindy's hair stood up on her arms. Cindy moved from the drink counter to the fridges under the security mirror—right up to the dirty man and with a finger pointed at the middle of his chest the words tumbled from her mouth.

"Like what you see?" She thought for a second and added, "Perv." Then she pulled up her skirt a bit. "Is that better?" She pulled one side up high and uncovered pale skin. The skin prickled next to the cold glass of the beer fridge.

He reached out a hand. She stepped back, slapped it, and shivered. There were two of her. Cindy felt like she was controlling herself without really controlling herself—as if one Cindy was sitting on the roof of the station peering down and the other Cindy was performing for this drunk. A puppet master and puppet all stitched together as one, she pulled the strings tight with one hand and watching the other hand pull the fabric of her skirt up her thigh.

She considered leaving the drunk alone, but she only considered it. "Dude," Cindy said. "Don't go getting all handsy."

Cindy knew she should just leave, but she didn't want to do that, so she said, "Meet me in the bathroom."

The drunk's eyes widened, and he let the glass case door bang closed on the white shelves of malt liquor. Cindy turned around and pushed out the gas station doors and turned around to the side where the cracked bathroom door looked out at the dumpster in the parking lot. A long black slit. Cindy threw the slushie at a coyote nudging at a ripped garbage bag next to the green dumpster sitting at the edge of the lights. She pushed the bathroom door open with her foot and stepped into the dark room.

Heavy rain followed the wind down from the mountains that night. The burst of wind at the front end swept the drunks away, garbage across a parking lot. They cradled their bottles against their bodies and bent over running for the comfort of a ditch or the shelter of the small bridge down the road. Cindy and Curtis were all alone.

The bathroom dripped wet. Cindy didn't know if it was from the door that didn't stay closed, always banging in the wind. It smelled sour just like a gas station bathroom.

"It's gross in here. Follow me, and maybe I'll let you touch me."

Cindy led old man Curtis out of the bathroom. Her hair clung to her shoulders. Curtis slipped on the rocks. His boots scraped. Cindy pulled her coat tight and didn't turn around. Leftover rain bounced against the plastic lid of the dumpster. He would follow her across traffic. Like a dog hounding a scent, Curtis could smell it. He wanted it. Cindy touched her coat pocket for a second. The beat of the rain pushed away the sound of the station and the two lane road and even Curtis's quick breathing in the tiny bathroom stall was just a memory.

"Here," Cindy said. She turned in front of a barbed wire fence, and she pulled her coat open with both hands. Dark spots polka dotted her white shirt. They spread and connected with each other.

"Curtis, I know I said you could touch me," Cindy said, "but I am going to be honest with you. I didn't really mean it." She pulled Grandmother's knife from a coat pocket.

Curtis hooked his finger around one of the buttons of her shirt.

"That knife's too big for a little girl."

Cindy pushed his hand back. Her shirt stuck to her skin.

Curtis grinned. "I can see through your shirt."

"I'm serious," Cindy said, "I decided something tonight."

"Okay," Curtis said. The dirt and rocks at their feet helped the night of drinking keep him unsteady. He reached out for her shirt again. He slipped and grabbed the fencepost instead.

Cindy shoved at Curtis with both hands. He caught her wrists with her hands on his chest and pulled her close. Curtis twisted the wrist with the knife, and it fell to their feet.

"I ain't drunk," he slurred. He turned her around in his arms and held her there with her back against his body. Her hair caught in his beard, and he breathed with his mouth open next to her ear. He smelled like spilled beer and spilled piss. The short breaths reminded her of the grunts men made working in tight spaces. Cindy knocked the back of her head into his face. Curtis put a hand on his jaw but held Cindy tight with the other. His arm clotheslined Cindy and pinned her to his chest. Cindy grabbed it with both hands and pulled her knees and balled up, hanging in the air. Her weight pulled him forward and they tumbled to the ground. They splashed into the mud.

Cindy felt the slippery edges of a rock sticking out of the dirt. She pulled at it with her fingertips. She swept her hands over the ground feeling for anything, another rock, her knife.

"I decided something too," Curtis said, "You're really pretty enough, but you remind me of somebody."

"Screw you, Curtis," said Cindy, "you're just a nasty old man."

Curtis rolled her over and put a hand under her shirt.

"Get your drunk ass off of me."

"I ain't drunk," Curtis said. His breath was hot on her neck. He unbuckled his pants and pushed them to his ankles.

"Get off of me," Cindy said.

Curtis smiled.

A bark interrupted Curtis. Beside them growled a big coyote.

Curtis rolled into the dirt away from the animal.

Curtis laughed, "Shit that scared me. Get out of here." He threw a handful of dirt in the direction of the animal.

The coyote stepped forward and stood still over Cindy. It stepped forward again. The hair hackled on its back, from its neck to the base of its tail. The skin of the animal shimmered in the rain. Instead of the rain falling off its coat, it looked like the skin itself dripped away. Even while it stood still, the skin shifted in place and stretched, but when Cindy stared at it nothing moved. She rubbed the rain from the corner of her eyes.

The coyote raised its head and barked twice. A high pitch met by nearby yips. Two more ragged creatures loped into view.

Cindy backed away from them. Dirt and mud squished between her fingers and she felt the steel of the knife. Her fingers curled into a fist around the handle.

"Quit staring at me." Curtis threw another clump of dirt at the animal. Curtis kicked a leg out untwisting his jeans, but he was balled up and shackled by his own pants.

The coyote turned its head. The eyes glowed, not like an animal's eyes when reflecting a car's headlights but there was the hint of color, of blood dripped into dirt. The creature stepped aside.

Curtis sank deeper into the mud, bound for slaughter.

Cindy's memory replayed something Grandfather said, "Okay, child, pull the blade here." His finger traced an imaginary line across the throat of the lamb.

Cindy stood up tall in the rain and wiped the tangled hair across her forehead with the back of her hand. She stepped forward and prepared the blade. She wiped it clean. She smeared mud from both sides of the long blade across her coat.

The road to school was bumpy. Cindy looked away from the rearview mirror down to her hands. Dirt dwelled deep under her finger nails. Every time she looked up, she met Grandmother's eyes in the rearview mirror. Cindy shivered on the warm green seat of the Oldsmobile.

She laid it out to the drunk the first time in the bathroom. "Here are the rules," she said, "no touching." The drunk broke the rules that night.

"Stop touching me."

"What?" Chicken Noodle wrinkled his forehead.

"What?" Cindy said.

"Not touching you," he said.

Cindy grabbed his hand.

Chicken Noodle pulled his hand away.

"You don't touch me," he said, and then he added. "I know what you do in that bathroom." He whispered the word bathroom.

"Sweetie," Cindy said, "Noodle."

"Leave me alone."

"Sweetie, it's not," Cindy whispered, "It's not what you think."

"Cindy," Chicken Noodle said, "I won't tell."

"I know." Cindy said. It is what people say with secrets. It is said sometimes when people don't know at all. I know is believable. It's not too convincing, but it's not without personality.

"I'll kill you if you ever tell anybody," Cindy's daddy used to whisper in the darkness.

"I know," Cindy said.

"I don't want to die," Curtis said last night in the mud and rain.

"I know," Cindy said.

Cindy revealed dirt from her fingernails. Grandmother's eyes reflected in the rearview mirror. They shifted color in the morning light. A bright orange glowed over the brown from those eyes as they took in the early morning sunlight.

"Cindy," Grandmother said, "When a butcher bird learns to hunt, she sticks to what she knows."

"I know," said Cindy. She continued to pick her fingernails, to unearth that dirt lodged just beneath the surface.

1952

My grandmother gave me my voice. I didn't want it. I had other plans. The people set roles and they were followed. I wanted a cloudy day, not this blue sky, not this light bed quilt spread over the frame of mesa rock. Our procession followed single file along the ridge of a river far below. The river cut through red rock, a blade of green grass trampled into the mud.

"Why can't we ride in a truck?" I asked.

"The sun rises every day, child," said my grandmother, "It is the way of things."

Turquoise lines in her loomed dress ran like rivers through the dark red wool.

"I am not the sun."

"You, child, are a two headed snake," whispered my grandmother. "You are not the sun."

"But why do we have to walk?" I rubbed my stomach. The heat of the day pushed heavy on my shoulders, and reached into my stomach.

Between our two families, one horse was spared for the move. Shame spared no one. The burning of Earl Tsosie might have been forgiven, if not forgotten, but the shaming of my family was too great a weight to forgive. Our night together, an act to dispel the burden of grief, to set George back on a path leading into the sun, paved the surface of our shame. Through this one misspent night, George and I condemned our entire families into the unknown of new lands.

Forgotten in thought, I stopped walking and tracked circles with my fingertips around my navel. Beside me, the wooden slats of the sled scratched and bumped along the rocky ground. The pine runners gouged sharp-edged rocks. A sweet smell, the smell of morning, the smell of the first growth of spring dotting hillsides green lifted from the pine.

I rubbed my leg muscles above my knees. We dragged sleds through a low gully. Behind us a line of nieces, nephews, aunts, and uncles stretched. The children dared each other to edge closer to the ravine. Ahead on the trail, George and my father chitted to each other. The harsh sound sheepherders made, their clinched teeth whistles cut through the noise of the herd between them. The sheep called out, too. They herded the flock up the hillside searching for grass. For now, the herd followed a cut down to our trail. The sheep nudged together, nosing each other forward, like an unorganized river of black and white they rolled over the terrain. Last night's rain matted their wool. The tangled wool matted with twigs and burrs and the last sheep lifted its tail and dropped pellets of shit on the trail.

"If we couldn't hear them, we could follow them by smell," I said.

"Varela, no. Do not say bad things," Grandmother said. She sucked her tongue from her teeth.

The path turned around a bend. Gravel the color of spilled blood moved at the scuffing of our feet. The continuous crunch of the sheep hooves on the gravel sounded a light percussion to the song of their bleating. The herd turned the bend and their crying and scampering quieted. An old tree leaned away from the edge of the ravine toward us.

"Stop," said my grandmother. She put her arm across my chest as if she were keeping me from stepping off the ravine.

The dragging crunch of the wooden sleds ended. The sound of the day rose around us. The tiny river to our side splashed with playful eddies. Chirps darted from the branches of the pines, the tiny peeps of warblers harvesting a hatching. Even the skitter of some tiny animal, a mouse maybe, caught my ear. From the tree a shadow moved, as if a limb was turning towards us.

A coyote stepped into view. Rain-filled nights painted the coyote's hide like the wool on the sheep. His yellow coat, dulled brown and red from mud, lay ragged across his shoulders. The skin was too tight, and his steps were short and quick, as if he felt uncomfortable in his own skin. The coyote turned his head. Eyes reflected the red dirt. Sniffing the air, he turned back. Like a dog, he tucked tail and disappeared around the tree.

"We should turn around also."

"But, grandmother, we will lose them," I said. I pointed to the bend in the path.

"When a coyote crosses your path, you turn around. If we follow the men, something terrible will happen."

"That is just a story, grandmother."

"There is no such thing as just a story."

Grandmother turned and talked to the other women. A couple of the children ran to the edge of the ravine and threw rocks into the air. The rocks arced over space and hung, for a moment, before plummeting out of sight.

Our two families left Arizona for government land in New Mexico. Because I had been promised to another family, to another man, our shame clung to us like the stink of shit on the trail. I didn't want anything, not a life with George, not the shame I carried, not the shirt clinging to my back where my bag rubbed and trapped my sweat from escaping into the dry desert air.

The sheep huddled into little puffs, little balls on the hillside. George slid down the bank. Rocks and dirt rolled around his leather shoes. The kicked up dirt reminded me of planting the garden in the spring. George moved with the grace of a mountain cat, sure footed even sliding down the bank, his lean body always in control.

"Here," he said. Two peeled cactus apples sat wet in his palm, the green fruit pocked from the sheered spines. His long hair stuck to his forehead and the sweat on his face looked like the glisten from the cactus fruit. His smile, always around the edges of his eyes, pulled now at the corners of his lips so that the white of his teeth shone through, winter snow hidden in the tanned landscape of his face.

"I don't want this," I said.

Before the sun dropped behind the horizon, we rolled out blankets and ate from a basket of piñons.

A short walk from where we stopped stood a thicket of short pine dark against the sky. I squatted. My pee splattered into a pool and a skinny stream cut between my splayed feet. The stream puddled before breaking through the dam of collected needles and spilling over a rock, out of sight. I sprinkled sandy dirt over the top of it, watching it soak up dark and earthy.

"We have the choice to cross its path," said my grandmother, "but it is taking a chance on bad luck."

"Is it just the coyote?" asked one of the children.

"That spirit can bring harm," said my grandmother. Her voice settled my thoughts and the stories and moments blended around me and disappeared.

In the darkness, voices shrieked across vast mesas. I opened my eyes. The wind was mocking me like it does. Then it became more than the wordless voice of the wind.

"We hear you," said the winds, "We are here for you. We hear you." The words brushed past, tangled my hair. "We hear you. We are here for you."

I pulled my shirttail over my head. When I opened my eyes, the fabric tickled my eyelashes. The voices faded, but the wind kept blowing.

The gray morning light is ubiquitous. It is dark, and then it is light.

"Grandmother," I asked. "Does the wind speak to you?" A shiver ran up my spine. The earth cooled at night and sucked me cold.

"No, child," she said, "the wind last spoke to the people when the gambler took everything we held dear."

"I don't mean in story."

"The answers are in story."

"But the wind is carrying words with it."

"No, child, the wind has not spoken since the days were new."

I twisted the end of my hair. Grandmother smiled with only her mouth. Her eyes stayed on my fingers. I stopped twirling my hair.

"Grandmother?"

She moved her eyes from my hair and we gazed at each other. Her dark eyes moved back and forth, the flicker of flame.

"What voice is it?" she asked.

"It is the voice of the wind. It says it hears me. It is here for me. It says it like the wind blows, in constant repetition."

"It is not the wind," she said.

"I hear it."

"Do not listen to the voices in these lands. We are traveling the edge of grounds that are not for this life. Do not listen to these voices."

"What do they want?"

"I do not know what they want with you, child. You are precious to me, but you are a different bird, you are a butcher bird, following your own way," she said. "It may be you are precious to another."

"George?"

Grandmother smiled again. Her fingers brushed my cheek. Her touch, the morning breeze.

"I will not always be here for you," she said, "Listen to yourself. When you hear voices on the wind, listen to yourself, but do not listen to a voice you do not know. George will need you. Watch over him, Varela. There is a reason behind everything, even shame." Her fingers crossed from my arm to my belly. She placed her hand flat, and I felt warm.

The wind tore across the desert floor. It knotted the tree limbs. My hair slapped and turned across my forehead. The stunted pines clung to the sides of the ravine. Whispers swirled like water.

"Are you awake?" asked George. His voice jumped out from the darkness. Rain rattled dry sticks at the edge of the flat where we were sleeping. He had slithered across the ground.

"Go away." I rolled over.

"I want to see you."

"Go away."

"I will love you, you know," he said. His fingers touched my hair.

"I will never love you." I swept his hand away.

"You will," said George. His mouth was at my ear. I felt his breath more than I heard his words.

My father stopped snoring.

"It will never happen," I whispered.

"You cannot know what will happen," said George. "You have only been taught the stories of the past, not the future." His lips touched my ear. The touch was light.

I shivered. "Don't presume to know me, future husband," I said.

"I will care for you," he said. He reached over me and placed his hand to my stomach. I rolled again. My blanket slipped from my bare legs. The chill crept along and prickled my skin.

"Yes, you will," I said.

Watch over him, I heard my grandmother's voice in my head.

"I will show you," he said. His warm hand rested on my thigh. He rubbed his thumb on my skin.

The steady breathing from my father settled into the beat of the night.

The chill didn't leave. "Go away." I closed my eyes. George lifted his hand. With a slide of his boots in the dirt, he was gone.

Later my father snored. "We hear you," said the voices. "We are here, we are here."

I wrapped my blanket around my shoulder and sat still trying to focus my eyes on the play of darkness and on the nothing that they saw.

The breeze pushed across the land as darkness. It built itself into a fury. It pushed forward ahead of the escaped day, ahead of the heat radiating from rocky runs and tossed boulders. The breeze was hair streaking across the sky caught up like a stringy buildup of clouds.

The wind shrieked a high pitched howl, a beast sitting everywhere at once and crying into the night from every direction. Flashes of lightning in the mountains illuminated the dark for a moment. The pines bent and swayed. Clothes and bedding rolled and caught in the branches at the edge of the clearing.

Voices spoke again, "We hear you, we hear you." The whine of the wind whipped the corners of the bed roll. It slapped against itself, the sound of my grandmother shaking out bedding in the morning.

"Here for you, here for you."

The white flash of lightning burst through the darkness and the bang of the storm neared.

With the wind lifting the edges of the bedroll and driving grit into my skin, I heard the rumble of a migrating herd in the distance. Maybe it was the shifting weight of a train bending along its iron rails.

The train neared. I squinted into the dark. There was no light. No stars, no moon, no single-eyed headlight searching the darkness. No lights of any kind, only the thunder of the nearing herd. The rumble neared the high ledge above us.

My father stopped snoring again early in the storm. He sat and turned his head toward me.

"What is that sound?" he said.

"Migration," I said.

His blanket dropped to the ground. He stood still for a moment with his head turned. He yelled, "Wake up."

All over the clearing the storm disturbed sleep and one of the younger children cried. His cry lifted and twisted into the wind and then ripped away into the night.

The rumble of tires shook the ground. The flat where we slept filled with runoff water from above.

The clearing turned into the wash of a new river.

My grandmother pushed me off my bedding and rolled it.

"No," yelled my father, "Leave it. Move up hill."

Grandmother yanked me to my feet. The roar of the nearby traffic turned into the crashing of waves. It was the mix of rain and water rushing ahead of a desert storm.

"Move!"

Water fell down the slope we were climbing. The surge brought its own wind, its own shrieking. I gasped and hid my eyes against my forearm. It fell heavy. It crashed, a never-ending wave of water slammed onto us from above. The children climbing the ledge in front of us slipped. Small arms slapped at the surface of water and rock. Their grips tore away from ledges and branches in an instant.

I reached, but my grandmother pulled me back up the slope, and then we both were swept off the hillside into the ravine.

The storm and rushing water layered black on black. The fall into the ravine surrounded me with liquid air, with screams, and bleats, and objects crushing together. My face smacked water's surface and the sting stole my breath. I sank into the arms of the river. The greedy fingers of the river's flow pulled at me, sucking my skirt to tangle around my legs. Although my knees wrapped in place with my skirt, I kicked and both legs pushed me to the surface in unison.

Water roared. White caps broke and slapped into old bent trees and giant boulders. In the dark the white spray fanned into the air like Coyote spilling a blanket of stars into the sky. The swirl of water edged the darkness and the two met and disappeared into each other, lovers unaware of the world, staying stranded in each other's arms.

The push of mud and roll of debris swept us from the flat to the edge of the rise into the furious boil of river below.

"Daughter, hold on." Grandmother reached for me, and then she spun away with the water.

Strong hands grabbed at me in the dark. George's fingers squeezed, raked my skin. The river pulled us apart. He dove towards me. I heard his body slap into the water. He swam up to me, a large fish circling my feet.

"Give me your hand," he said. He grabbed my sleeve and pulled.

The cloth stretched, and again my feet swept from under me, and again he reached out to me. His other hand grabbed the shirt, and it pulled over me releasing me into the rage again.

The fight to breathe, the fight to keep my head above the surface, to stop slamming into underwater boulders and rocks, took me from George. The fight was all I had. Every time my knees crunched into a boulder I sucked air and sank below the surface.

George was at my side again. His warm hands pulled me at my

waist, pulled me toward him and toward the edge of the rage, out of the river.

"Let me go!" I screamed. "Let me go." I scratched his face. I clawed at him, an angry cat. The welts from my nails would burn red on his face and arms in the morning, if morning found us at all.

The river roared in the ravine. Branches tumbled out of the dark pulled along back into the dark. Trees floated past, giant arthritic fingers reaching and grabbing anything.

George dragged me to the shore. The water on the sides pooled and swirled. It shifted, searching, always searching for a new tributary to follow, a new crevice to fill.

Splashing to shore, I wept. The terror of the dark, the screams of the dark, and the unknown of the dark squeezed its claws around my heart. I shivered.

"We hear you. We hear you."

I screamed into the darkness.

George wrapped his arms around me. He pulled me into the hollow of his body. Where did his warmth come from? River water and sand stuck to our skin and his smell comforted me, like the warmth of a fire early in the morning.

"It is okay now."

"No, let me go."

"I can't."

"Let go, let me go. I don't want to be here."

"I will not. I cannot."

"I don't want life anymore."

There was no one else. No more screams, no more water rushing around us, no more rain. Everything was quiet. Our skin stuck together. George held me tight. His chest expanded against my back with his breathing.

The wind began again later in the night. It cried around me.

George's heavy breathing pushed my breasts against his arms. With every breath his arm brushed my skin.

In the early morning hours, in the dawn when the light of the sun begins to lift the darkness, they walked around us.

"We will hold you. We will guide you. We will carry you through the world." A chorus of voices, like far off wind in the valleys surrounded us.

"I don't want you," I said.

"You need us," they said. "Give us voice and we will give you body."

I wanted to stand, to wake George, but I was paralyzed, imprisoned in George's embrace.

The chorus of voices settled into three long-legged shadows.

The shadows spoke in unison.

"We will guide you," they said. "We will carry you."

Every leaf, every pine needle hung limp in the clearing. The river moved without haste around the debris of the night.

"We will give you body."

The voices collected and the middle shadow spoke. The sound of iron on rock, the sound of scraping and imprisonment welled behind the words. The air twisted around us, a dust devil spun to life and the river and the trees on the ledges disappeared behind a curtain of grit. We sat isolated in the eye of a wind storm.

They all spoke again, voices in unison.

"Give us your voice."

One settled, melted into itself, and the run and drip of the melt molded into scales and a large shadow snake coiled and flicked its tongue. The eyes two pricks of red. It slipped up my body and leaned off of my shoulder and flicked its tongue at George. The tongue flicked across George's lips, and the snake levered itself over and wrapped its body around George's neck. The tongue flicked the air at George's ear.

The middle shadow dropped onto all fours and grew into the shape of a mountain cat before twisting into a large coyote. The head of the beast dropped. It sniffed the air. Eyes the color of red earth lifted, and the beast raised a howl into the din of the windstorm.

The last shadow melted and the drips turned to feathers and a large owl turned eyes of coal ember, unblinking, to me. The owl spread its wings and flew into the middle of the whirlwind.

"Give us your voice," they said. The snake around George's

neck slipped around my neck. "Give us your voice," it said into my ear.

"Go away," I cried.

It sank its fangs into my neck.

I screamed. George didn't move. I couldn't move. I needed to move. I wanted it.

The fire of its poison rushed to my heart. I felt it swell through my veins with every heartbeat. The pain gathered at my heart. The shriek of the wind returned until I realized it was my own voice inside of the swirling wall of dirt and wind.

"You have it," I screamed, "You have it." The sun broke the edge of the horizon. Light blistered along the mesas. The dust settled and the shadows fled from the bright light.

George woke. We looked along the river bed. Empty, as if my family had been a dream. Wedged between branches the wet wool of sheep dotted the river.

The bleat that met our ears led us to sheep who escaped the flash flood. The tangle of legs and wool pocked the mud-banks along the river.

Three small carvings lay in the dirt where we waited out the night. I picked up the wooden owl, his tufted ears pointed and watchful, and then the coyote sitting back on his haunches with his snout lifted in a howl, but I hesitated with the slender coiled snake wrapped in a circle, eating his tail. Owl and coyote helped the people, helped watch for the twins in story.

There is no story of the snake.

"Let's go," George said. "We need water and clothes. We have a long way to go. We need each other."

"For now," I said.

I don't know why I did it, but I slipped that taboo, the circlet of the snake figurine, over my hand. The wooden scales shifted on my wrist. This story didn't exist. It didn't make sense, and now I was alone. I crossed my arms over my bare chest and followed George towards the bleating.

Before Following Your Vengeance,
Dig Two Graves

Air whispered from the mountain. The stretched range was heavy in shadow except for the eastern ridges uncovered by sunlight. The sloped foot of the mountain shifted into flats. A power line pulled across the brown terrain to a rise where crows called back and forth. They landed in the branches of a bent pine. A small house sat on the rise.

At the kitchen window, a guttered candle had gone cold, extinguished in the pooling of its own wax. A single steel needle jutted from the belly of the red stub. A tiny wooden owl perched next to the candle. It watched the other side of the windowsill. Three small horned lizards laid side by side. Their long-ways cut stomachs revealed tiny ballooned organs settled in the morning air and in the way of death. The Loggerhead Shrikes caught the devils and barbed them on the thorn bushes at the edge of the yard. The shrikes policed the yard from the barbed wire strung along the far edge by the cluster of pine bent toward the east. They sat during the heat of day, their curved beaks half open, panting like a litter of porch hounds.

The kitchen was warm. A pot of water simmered on the stove top. The water bounced. At the table, an old woman twisted herbs into tight bundles. Her fingers rolled the fibers together. Through the window, she watched the morning.

"They will steal your eyes," she said.

Varela saw death. She saw it in the glassy reflection of her morning tea. She saw it in the bloat of the bellies on her window sill. She saw it every day. Today, it carried the weight of sorrow heavy in its arms. The kitchen window glowed from the morning light pushing its way into the dark house.

She was often drawn to the window of the room by the light of morning. When her daughter was young and her husband at war, she spoke words and wove them into the air, into the light—and her mind became a great owl with great wingspan. It left through the opening and crossed oceans and jungles into the dark side of the world and then back out of it again. With a few beats of her wings, Varela arrived. She landed and sometimes slipped into the easy shape of a fox where from shadows she watched George as he sank further, step by step, into rice flats.

She watched him from the edge of the forest while he lay in the muck and shivered. She watched him let the family burn, watched him turn his back and let the tree spear a soldier through the heart.

After the accident, she sat at the jungle edge and stared at the green canvas of his tent. He struggled to breathe the heavy air of Vietnam, so she watched over him.

George coughed and the eave timbers popped. Chicken Noodle slept. Most of the world still rested, but the morning brought crows down from their perches in the mountains and the trees shifted under their weight. The crows settled the branches as she opened the front door.

"Crow, what you want with me today?" she asked. Her voice cracked hoarse in the early morning.

The loose murder picked their feathers and turned their heads but held their voices. They watched her turn the soil. Maybe it was the early hour or maybe the significance of the morning, but something stilled their arguing. Their black eyes followed her movement.

She picked at some rows dipping her fingers into the night-cooled earth. She stood often and placed fists into the small of her back and arched looking up into the leftover stars in the sky. The early morning tend of the garden pulled at her back in the same way a child in her womb had pulled at her back, and her garden was temperamental in the same way Kaila had been spoiled.

Sometimes cycles begin on a day where the calendar of events cannot be ignored. George said something close to that when he boarded the bus at the beginning of 1963. That bus took him to the jungles of Vietnam.

"Take care of the girl," he said, "It is time." His breath puffed into the air as he said girl, and then he kissed Kaila on the cheek. The bus pulled from the side of the road, and Varela stood holding their little girl's hand. George left her standing in their life and nothing changed when he returned.

Bent over the soil, she pulled stubborn roots, and she kept in her mind the still tangle of memory—the laughter and tears of a child grown old. She and her daughter left the bus stop and walked to the pickup that cold day. She explained war as best she could. The tears she didn't have ran down her daughter's face for days and weeks after he left. Both the tears and the laughter faded then. The tears and laughter faded now. All she had left of her daughter was an image now in her memory of a finch or a sparrow hopping along a fence, looking and peeking and endlessly curious, that was how she remembered her daughter. The image of a songbird replaced the braided image of Kaila. The braids were too short or too long ago to grab a hold. She could not pull her daughter's face into focus anymore, could not pull it into the front of her mind anymore, because merciless time changed and muted the memory-image of those braids and that child-face into thought, into an abstract of emotions and words.

Varela nourished an overwhelming desire for all these years. From a seed of unbelievable agony into a shoot of vengeance, her old body birthed another child. Thirteen years of water and light and soil and her vengeance, that thing, rooted deep inside her. It began with the twisted bundles of green thread tea she wrapped for George. She twisted them with quick jerks so the bundles did not loosen in water and twisted them with climbing nightshade so his coughing and stomach ache did not end before she decided what to do with him. He drank the tea because he believed it relieved his pain. Everyone believed Varela in these matters.

"Where were you?" she whispered looking past her shoulder in the direction of distance. "Where were you?"

After working the garden and sweeping the front, she went back inside and poured the last of the hot water into a thermos. She placed the thermos back down on the kitchen counter. Pinned behind it a handful of faded valentine cards stuck to the wall. Varela unpinned the first one, crumpled and small. They were all brown hearts. The first time Chicken Noodle gave her one, the one in her hands, he worried the color would bother her. She told him the color was more like the real thing. And in a way the uneven cut edges almost took on the shape of a real heart. He brought her a brown heart every February now, and every year they were cut out with more precision. She didn't have the heart to tell him the first one, the crooked one, was her favorite.

Chicken Noodle was a good boy. He minded. He kept to himself. The garden wasn't his favorite place, but what young boy gardens with his grandmother? No, he was a good boy. He was her joy.

She placed the thermos on the table and pulled the rusted tin of tea bundles out and left it on the table too. The handle from the long kitchen knife on the counter found its way into her hand. She placed the smooth handle of the blade into her shoulder bag. Yesterday, in the evening, she packed a jar of ash into the bag and a bottle of water and a worn carving of a round-bellied owl. Its tufted ears rubbed low—rubbed low long before the wooden creature found its way to her.

Her fingers tickled the leaves of the herbs and plants by the window. She considered something. It was a moment she had not allowed herself for the past thirteen years, because Kaila's journey was important—anybody's last journey was important—and because she did not want to anchor her daughter in the here and in the now. The here. The now. It was all too heavy, so a tug, like a string attached to her womb, pulled her from the house.

The crows in the wind-bent pine watched her go. Silent, they stayed their perch.

Varela passed the rocks behind the house and turned north toward the mountains. The sun pointed her way. It crossed over her shoulders and cast a companion to her left. She walked in the quiet company of the sun with her duality struggling along the broken terrain beside her. The shadow rolled over the rocks and desert bushes like a flash flood covering and quickly leaving its path.

The sun reached its fingers far across the sky. She neared the mountain foot. She walked uphill for hours, remembering a way not walked in years.

Another string attached to her stomach. George came home that late afternoon years and years ago and found their daughter motionless and dying on the couch.

"We have to figure out how to forgive ourselves," George said.

"What if I cannot forgive you," she said to the memory. Her hand shielded her eyes. She blinked into the sinking sun. "What if I do not want to forgive you?"

The day moved past her. She did not notice the heat or the distance or the walking. Memory insulated her from all the passing.

The sun pulled darkness out of the earth. It sank away along the western horizon. She placed a hand on her flat, shrunken belly. It had just been she and George here so many years ago. He swept their footsteps away, and she remembered the fallen boulder hunched like the shell of a great turtle where he burned the wooden stretchers, the crude shovel, and the bunch of dried thorns he used to broom their tracks. She remembered the gray smoke whip around them and sting their eyes and how the unwelcomed tears from the smoke streaked the ash covering George's face. They walked home, and she carefully wiped her own cheeks clean. The white smudges on her fingertips reminded her of Kaila and Kinaalda and a time without George, a time when her memory of their daughter remained safe from his mistakes.

The boulder sat before her. This moment was unique. Again, she knew no stories to guide her. She took the jar from her bag and rubbed ash along her arms, and neck, and the boney places of her face. The back of the great rock split open, just as cracked and red as she remembered. She leaned against it. Her weight pushed the skin of her palm into the roughness of its crust. The tumble of desert brush changed. Everything in her memory served change, the only constant master. The years of growth and storms and time itself changed the flat behind the boulder into what looked like any stretch of desert.

A movement at her hand took her attention away from the cycles of time. A skinny shadow emerged from a crevice in the rock.

"Snake," she said, "you have come as well." A moment passed between the two.

The sun's heat still radiated from the sandstone. The snake's eyes, a pair of inside out stars floating across a white sky, sucked up time unblinking. The snake coiled back. It began to slip into the secret places of the boulder. From there it might try and twist the lines out of Eden's navel.

Maybe too many years passed waiting for an answer or maybe the thin slender body reminded her, steered her into a deep cave, a place once marked with desire—a place of emptiness except for the mask of her own boulder which sat alone and which she carried with her every day.

"Snake," she said, "you should not have come."

It did not move.

Varela snatched it. She grabbed the rattlesnake from its back, just above the rattle. Her movement quick like a cat hunting mice in summer grass. She clutched the tiny body and yanked him from his hole. The snake's head drifted inches from the ground and he tasted only dirt with the flick of his tongue.

Just as the snake flexed its powerful stomach, she grabbed its head and brought the twisting body to her face.

"You should have prepared two graves, snake," she said, "When you sank your poison into my family. You should have feared leaving me untouched."

Bending the neck towards her mouth she sank her teeth into the tough stranded tissue of its muscles. She bit down hard. A crack joined the increased curls of the snake's skin brushing her arms, and the jerk of its body met her clenched teeth. She squeezed her jaws together.

Muscle juice stringing her chin, Varela pulled the snake away from her mouth. Spitting flank of flesh, she snapped the spine completely with a twist of her hands. She swung the body by the tail and whipped it across the boulder's back and she beat the snake's body against the boulder.

The cool twilight air settled still to watch. The snap of skin on rock cracked the silence. Again and again the tattered body slapped against the red sandstone. The wind held its breath.

Both hands fixed to the end of the slick body. She whipped it over and over until the flesh and skin released and the ragged body burst and disintegrated into the air. It landed around her like a gravely rain.

She sucked air over the back of her teeth. Her shoulders dropped down and she sucked in air again.

A coyote call brought her back into her mind. Her right hand held the rattle-end of the snake with tufts of pink muscle flayed out of her fist. An answering call yipped from high on a cliff above.

The sun followed its path behind the mountains so the brightness of the moon started its rise. She breathed and pushed bits of hair back behind her ears. The ash on her arms streaked with sweat and snake. She trembled in the quiet and let herself fall to her knees.

"Mother," a quiet voice said.

Varela turned her head left and right to look over both shoulders. She was alone.

"Daughter," she said, "Kaila."

Her knees pressed the desert floor. She took out the kitchen knife from her old weaved bag. She squinted at the mirrored moon. With the turn of her wrist, the moon bounced off the blade and sprang into her eyes. Her other hand felt her stomach, her empty stomach. The tip of the blade found her navel. The blade craned its neck as if it was an animal sniffing her life, her origin, her power.

"Mother, this is a mistake."

"No, my daughter."

The wind waited before moving down the slope.

"I have been to the end of the earth, I have been to the end of the waters, I have been to the end of the sky, and now I am here at the end of the mountains and I, I have found none that are my—"

"Mother," with the third calling of her woman-name she pulled the point of the knife from her belly and sank the blade into the ground. Her fingers smudged dust from the metal shine. Her eyes met the dulled eyes in the snake head. It lay there discarded. She leaned forward, picked up the detached thing. The front teeth glistened.

"Yes, Daughter, yes," she rubbed the severed head. She rubbed between the eyes with her thumb, "Yes, you are right. It is a mistake."

The Moon crept higher into the sky. It strained its great eye to watch the old woman kneeling on the desert earth way down below, trying to understand the story unfolding in its light.

"Your father chose long ago, did he not?" She turned the decapitated head in her hand. "He chose his own family. He chose over you and me. That was the mistake. He is the one who has lived too long. It is not me."

The bundled tea was cruel. Where was her justice in it? The years of silence were cruel. Without a word, she whittled the man down to a poorly crafted carving, to something useless and thrown into the fire so it burned up to be no more.

"Kaila."

The tender scent of the snake's open body floated away into the night as the wind moved. The smell of memory. It reminded her of stories when she was young, of stories when the people were young.

"Forgive me," she said and stood and repeated, "Forgive me."

Leaving the blade in the ground, an exchange of sorts, Varela put the head into her bag. She placed it with care in the bottom corner. For the second time in her life, she left the turtle-backed boulder and the quiet foot of the mountain. Her mind stayed with the past, with stories so old they were less than memories and more images without words.

Her own footprints followed her down the slope away from the boulders and mountains and the scattered snake. The desert space shifted long and quiet under a low sound. A sound enveloped the nighttime, piercing—the bark of a coyote but steady like the wail of ridge wolf.

Varela hummed and rubbed the tufts of the wooden owl. The mountains disappeared faster than they appeared and the sliding space between time, between her footsteps, increased until she walked as if she were floating, until the landscape blurred and then, it happened in a couple of steps, she stood before the front door of her house. The Moon's position rested in the same spot when moments ago she rocked back and forth on her knees, the knife handle in her hands, its point leaning on her stomach.

Outside, the air played warm and comfortable. Inside occasional laughter spilled from an open window. He taught the boy all the secrets of the desert that his father and his father's father taught him. Tonight, the laughter sounded empty in her ears. George stole her laughter, like Coyote stole the Sun and Moon. He stole her life like Coyote stole the lives of the people so long ago.

"A mistake is swift."

She realized it. It all swam together. The muddy waters of spring turned clear and calm when the mountain runoff ended in early summer. It would release him, release the pain. Walking away from the house in the silver of moonlight she walked until she no longer heard the laughter. She walked because she knew her choice changed and she did not want to meet it yet.

"No, no, no," she whispered, "It is too much."

Varela grabbed her hair, she fell to her knees, and she rocked forward until her forehead touched cool earth. There are mistakes that follow mistakes that change the color of landscape forever. She lifted her head and looked across the desert. It was white. As far as she could see white painted the black silhouettes of her life. There was no image of her life to be. Varela cradled her belly with her arms.

"Kaila. Forgive me."

When the light quit from the windows of the house, she rose to her feet.

The house sat still in the early morning again. An unfinished game sat on the table. Shoes kicked off by the door and dishes held their water in the sink for the last time.

George's tea tin laid open on the counter. The bundles she wrapped rested across each other. The tin needed refilling soon.

"It will help you sleep," she will say again. She will say it again and again. It will be a comfort.

George coughed. The wrinkles on Varela's cheeks bunched together. She moved to Chicken Noodle's room. The child slept facing moonlight. His dark hair swirled her memory. His cheekbones and nose were straight like his mother's.

"Grandson," said Varela.

From her bag, she lifted the severed head of the rattlesnake into the dark of the room. She set the fangs at the pulse of skin on her grandson's neck. Streaks formed through the desert dust and the white ash on her cheeks.

Varela pressed the sharp barbs of venom into her grandson's neck. His eyelids opened and he pulled away. He looked past Varela and his eyes widened. The snakehead fell beneath the surface of the covers, a secret succumbing to the waves, to the depths of that quilted ocean.

Chicken Noodle put a hand on his neck. He rubbed the pricked holes with his fingertips and blinked. Her daughter's dark eyes hid in her grandson's stare. With his other hand, he touched her cheek.

"Grandmother," he said, "why are you crying?"

The Hunter

The man in the sunglasses grabs his things from the motel counter and walks to the door. The sun is a forgotten part of the sky. It is either behind a cloud or low on the horizon hidden by a mesa or a building. The light is soft, and no shadows jump out around the man. Shadows are forever linked to a source. If there were any shadows stretched out lazy on the pavement, they would be like signposts pointing backwards and saying, "There, there it is. There's the sun. It's been here all along."

The man in the sunglasses always rents the room for a day. He is a thin man. He wears a mustard shirt buttoned to his neck. Rings, bracelets, and a necklace cling to him in silver and turquoise.

Chicken Noodle recognizes him. The man in the sunglasses often trespasses here. He pauses in the opening of the motel office door and turns his head. The slow movement, head turned sideways, is of a man listening for something imperceptible. At this moment, Chicken Noodle is aware of his own participation and senses the man in the sunglasses is aware of him, too.

The sallow desk clerk tells his girlfriend on the phone, "This Jeffrey Dahmer type just checked in. He wears a lot of silver." The desk clerk is a chubby unshaven man.

Chicken Noodle is sure it is not Jeffrey Dahmer renting the room. He has no idea what Jeffrey Dahmer looks like, but he knows he is not the man in the sunglasses. Chicken Noodle tries to influence the clerk's thoughts, but every time the situation replays the clerk calls his girlfriend and tells her about Jeffrey Dahmer.

Again the clerk gives the man in the sunglasses room 213. Again the phone at the front desk rings.

"I am sorry to hear that, Ma'am." The clerk always says it just as Chicken Noodle knows he will.

The clerk dials the room for the man in the sunglasses, and Chicken Noodle hears the distant voice say, "lo." The man in the sunglasses often swallows the first part of a word.

The clerk suggests he be quieter. "The walls are thin," he says.

Later, the man in the sunglasses checks out. The clerk watches him drive away in his Buick Roadmaster, and then he takes a metal ring of keys and walks outside and up to the second floor. He twitches his hand and the keys bounce against each other, a wind chime without melody.

Chicken Noodle is usually stuck, hovering. Tonight, he follows the desk clerk out the door. Has he tried that before? Just walking out the door? Chicken Noodle discovers new secrets of interfacing with his dreams every night. It is a complicated and endless video game.

Tonight, being pulled along like a kite tethered to the waddling clerk, Chicken Noodle can feel his heartbeat quicken as the pair make their way to the second floor. He needs to know what is in the room.

They pass peeling door after peeling door. The yellowed paint is thick and smooth to the touch but lumpy from all the coats the metal doors have been given over the years. Each room has big double windows with dark curtains pulled shut on the inside. Chicken Noodle notices that he, like a vampire, has no reflection in the big picture windows. The air conditioners grumble and drip. Dark spots of concrete, like almost empty lakes, collect the moisture that pools underneath each unit.

Chicken Noodle stops following the clerk after turning the corner on the landing.

A massive coyote materializes before them. Chicken Noodle doesn't see the coyote at first, and then there it is as if it had been there all along. It is abstractly big, a hulking bear, and with lowered head, dark hidden eyes, and rippling skin it stands in the middle of the landing. The ragged skin shifts on its back.

The clerk walks past the disarranged animal as if he does not see it, and the coyote ignores the clerk in the same way. The coyote does see Chicken Noodle. The animal is breathing heavy and growls—low rumbles join the percussion of the air conditioners. The rumbles are deep and convey the size of the animal even if coyote's whining yips and barks are usually much less threatening although eerie and ghostly when Chicken Noodle wakes to them in the middle of the night.

A ridge of fur stands along the line of the coyote's back. The ridge, a low parapet, rises from its neck to the base of its stiff tail.

Chicken Noodle steps to the motel wall and shifts weight forward on his feet. His hands hang at his side, palms out toward the beast.

Ahead, the clerk stops at the door of the room.

The Coyote swings its eyes in Chicken Noodle's direction. The brow of the animal casts a shadow over them. It wears its skin as if it were a coat it could take on and off.

Chicken Noodle takes another step forward, and although the room beckons, the coyote with a rumble vibrating from its chest, steps toward him and lifts its head so Chicken Noodle can see the white ivory of its teeth. The growl's tone changes to a quick snarl—a warning.

He sees the clerk, down the landing, move into the room, and almost at once step back out of the room. The clerk closes the door and quickly shuffles, a half walk half run, back down the landing.

Chicken Noodle backs away from the menacing coyote with his arms still down and hands out as if balancing a tightrope just like his grandfather would with an agitated animal, and then he follows the clerk down to the office looking back over his shoulder, but the coyote doesn't follow them.

At the front desk, his light hair stuck in dark clumps to his sweaty forehead, the clerk picks up the telephone and after dialing a number drums a pencil back and forth on the counter and then says, "I need a police officer."

Chicken Noodle knew he had been dreaming. He knew like any-one might know. Bright morning sun and several incessant knocks woke him. At first, the sound circles his periphery, a mountain lion stalking its prey, and then it is a mouse scratching at some beam in the walls over and over, and then finally Chicken Noodle knows what it is: a wood pecker claw deep on the wooden side of the house testing a spot with short raps. Sleep, with its unending explanations, gave way to waking and the duller reality of the knocking became a knocking at the front door.

"Officer," he heard his grandmother say from the front stoop.

Their voices blended into conversation and gave way to the many other noises of early morning.

Chicken Noodle shielded his eyes from the bright morning sun, and he stared at the hop-trees, leaves playing in the sunlight and air, huddled outside his bedroom window, and decided he would go for a hunt.

Grandmother would make up her mind against it.

"You shouldn't," she would say, "not with everything that's taking place."

"Nothing's going on." He would say.

"It's dangerous."

"It's dangerous," he would then echo. There were times he often just repeated what she said. She found it disrespectful. He found it funny.

He wouldn't say he had a strange dream. That thought he would keep to himself. What he also might not mention was that he had been having a similar dream all summer. He was part of the story in different ways. Tonight brought, in front of the coyote, one of the rare occasions where he had any interaction with the others wandering across the landscape of his mind. He was often apart from the inner narrative, and he tried to understand his role or perspective. The dreams changed, like episodes of a TV show, and sometimes they were the same repeats on TV when you were actually excited for a new episode because usually you had to watch what Grandfather watched and that was reruns of Walker Texas Ranger.

His grandparents were old school. Grandfather worked a grave-yard shift, a night watchman, and was mostly absent. He worked nights and slept days. Grandmother kept to herself. There were those nights though, after waking from a dream, where he would stand up, wander the house, and discover she wasn't there.

"Noodle," she'd say the next morning, "you must not have seen me in all the covers."

He knew she had not been there. But he never heard her come, and he never heard her go. When he tried to crawl back into sleep, he listened to the wind, he imagined the wings of a great owl gliding parallel with the desert floor eyes searching, this way and that, for prey. That great owl soared on the lip of the wind and lingered in his memory as he fell asleep. Sometimes he thought he might be an owl sitting from an imaginary perch watching the unfolding of his story sublimate his subconscious.

From time to time, as Chicken Noodle was growing up, gossip of dark and unspoken things passed between his grandmother and her friends. They got together and worked on a broken loom or swapped stories, drinking green thread tea from the sprigs of herbs he and his grandmother wrapped into tiny bundles every spring. Some nights he stood outside the main room needing to pee but afraid they might see him. He watched their stretched reflections from the window opposite them. They sat in close together and talked. It was always the same three women.

He often overheard his grandmother say, "There is a way to fix everything that happens." These women did things. They weren't medicine men. They weren't men, but they fixed things.

This morning he met his grandmother in the kitchen carrying a tray of herbs from the window. She placed the tray on a spread of newspaper covering the table. The same bold headline which had come to define the summer: San Juan Killer Eludes Police.

Grandmother was thin and bent. Her long hair collected, black like darkness, in a loose coil on her head. The way she walked reminded Chicken Noodle of a desert animal picking its way past thorns and hot rocks and other obstacles littered across the desert.

Deadheading the rosemary, her fingers pinched through the tiny branches snapping off dried blooms and browned sprigs. The top of the dark soil in each pot jumbled with bits of fingernail clippings and tiny stones and pebbles. Pieces of glass and turquoise jutted from the soil like wind hewn monuments isolated from the sheer cliffs of each pot's round edge.

He realized he and his grandmother were in the middle of the conversation he imagined while lying in bed. He didn't remember the beginning of it, and was unsure of what he had just said. It was no different than coming out of a daydream during class. She took her eyes from the plants and the blackness of them cautioned him to reveal his next thought with care.

"It is dangerous," his grandmother said. The lines around her eyes were bunching up on themselves as she squinted at her grandson.

"More than we understand is happening in the desert."

"Does that have to do with the officer this morning?"

"No, Noodle, that was something else." Her fingers stilled for a moment.

Grandmother," he said. He held a wooden broom handle in his hands, swishing at the floor between his feet. He had known this conversation would take place. "It will just be for the day. I'll be back before dark."

"Why today?" she asked.

"Why today. No reason, just want to be out," he said. He let out a long shoulder slumping breath.

He leaned the broom back into the corner behind the swing of the door. At night, he swept the front yard. He swept from the Oldsmobile to the house. He swept away leaves and gravel all the way up to the stoop under the eave. His grandfather laughed when Chicken Noodle told him about sweeping the yard, but said he better do as his grandmother asked.

"You could drive me," Chicken Noodle said. He made circles with the tip of a finger on the glass pane in the front door. He could see a faint reflection of his face in the glass. His cheeks and chin were smooth. Black hair framed his face hanging down around his jaw line. He leaned in until he couldn't see his face anymore, until it disappeared and he could barely see his own brown eyes reflect back, and then he blew a warm breath, breath from deep inside him, onto the cool surface until it clouded. The circles he had been tracing with his finger, around and around, didn't cloud over completely and a wobbly spiral emerged to replace his face from the foggy glass.

"Noodle," his grandmother said, "this discussion is over. Until we know what it is, I don't want you out there alone."

"I know."

"You know that."

"I know that." Chicken Noodle traced the outline of a pair of glasses onto the surface of the window, onto the face of the wobbly swirl, "Grandmother?"

Her fingers stilled, for a moment, while tending her herbs.

"Did you hear breathing last night?" he asked.

"Breathing?"

"Breathing." Chicken Noodle nodded and said, "It was next to the hop trees. I heard it in the leaves. Then it knocked into my bedroom wall breathing and when I looked out I saw a shadow."

"You were dreaming," she said, "anyway, it's good you could see a shadow." She always said he was dreaming. Once he told her about the coyote he watched from his bedroom window. He explained the shifting silver skin in the moonlight. She listened to the coyote story, but she dismissed it as a creature born of imagination. When he chose to tell her about things like the coyote, things that actually happened, she labeled them dreams. Now that he stopped retelling them, he felt they were somehow mixed up with, or connected to the bodies in the desert, to the man in the sunglasses.

The drunks they found in the desert were really dead. The Navajo police were spread thin. The summer months were over. The killings were still happening.

"Could that have been—" Chicken Noodle let the question tail off. He squeegeed the foggy glass with the tip of his finger.

"A dream," she finished.

Chicken Noodle shook his head but didn't say anything.

Some nights the gas station is busy. The buildings around it sit still, somehow further in the distance than the mountains rising up on all sides. Like white clay stuck in the edges of a wooden floor, the mountains are outlined in the dark.

Chicken Noodle is always tied up in the back of a station wagon.

He can see his grandmother and her friends through the back hatch.

Silver duct tape is wrapped around his ankles and wrists and around his head covering his mouth. Lying on his side, he sees the man in the sunglasses at the pump. He appears, a reflection through the curved back window of the station wagon, like an actor moving into the center of a frame. Leaving the nozzle of the pump in the tank the man walks over to his grandmother who is selling burritos out of her Oldsmobile.

"Gyaaa," Chicken Noodle warns her, "gyaagyaa." The duct tape filters his speech into muted long vowel sounds. His taped wrists and ankles are together behind his back. He twists his wrists, but the stiff tape holds. He pulls at his feet. It is like trying to get out of a stiff pair of hiking boots without untying them. The tape holds.

So he kicks both feet. Instead of kicking the inside of the car for attention his kicking silently and only slightly rocks the back of the wagon.

He kicks out until his skin is wet with sweat. Breathing is difficult with the duct tape gag, and he stops often to carefully breathe through a gap at the corner of his mouth. The back windows begin to fog. Chicken Noodle leans his head to the side.

A group of people stand around his grandmother, and from his prone position in the back of the wagon he hears familiar voices.

"You know that's what I've been hearing too."

"The tracks are coyote tracks. The right size too."

The man in the sunglasses scratches his orange touk. Chicken Noodle recognizes the touk. It is his toboggan, his touk, his birthday present from his grandfather: an orange Carhartt touk with matching gloves.

"Might be related to that serial killer," an old man says, "read about him in the paper again," he leans back against the Oldsmobile, arms crossed, and kicks the tire with the back of his boot. "If it's him or not out here, it doesn't matter, he's going to pay when they catch him."

A few others nod.

The man in the sunglasses turns his head, listening. He holds out his hand to Chicken Noodle's grandmother but keeps his head tilted, "How much?" he asks.

"Gyaagyaagyaaa," Chicken Noodle yells through the duct tape. He kicks and thrashes in the back of the wagon.

Chicken Noodle knows his grandmother is about to notice the orange touk or maybe hear his duct taped cries from the station wagon.

He rocks the station wagon harder and knocks on the back window with his forehead, but no matter what he does he can't capture the attention of his grandmother or the others standing around her.

Every night defeat clings to him like beads of sweat and no one ever notices.

Grandmother tells him it was because it was just a dream. He once heard her tell somebody how a looped dream was a warning and that there was always a way out of it.

His grandmother looked at him from the kitchen table waiting for a response. "Daydreaming is ugly," she usually said. Not even. Was it possible to daydream an already dreamed dream? Chicken Noodle wanted to tell her about the man in the sunglasses and the convoluted dreams. How to begin?

"We have work today," his grandmother motioned her head to the window by the garden. She cupped her hand and swept the clippings from the tabletop into one of her herb pots. She stood, frowned at Chicken Noodle and walked out the door without saying another word. A patch of corn with a row of sunflowers grew green and strong all summer, but now, late in the year, the bright yellow faces of the sunflowers hung downcast and ragged and picked over by finches, and over the last week he and his grandmother cut and bundled the stalks.

Grandmother walked to the side of the coop where the hand tools leaned. Chicken Noodle grabbed a leftover burrito from the counter and his backpack from the floor and after a glance out the back window he walked out the front door, away from his grandmother, to the road. It was a short walk down to the gas station, and there he would see about getting a ride into the desert.

Chicken Noodle made no bones about it. He liked hitching. He wasn't sure if he liked to hitch for hitching's sake or if the freedom just helped count down the days to his driver's license.

Hitching wasn't bad from town. It was a small community and everyone knew Chicken Noodle, and everyone knew he hitched.

His orange touk made him stand out. He wore it all year long. Most everybody in town stopped to give him a ride as they turned south toward the interstate. It was hard to mistake Chicken Noodle in his orange touk.

Town was that same clump of buildings from his dreams. It sprouted from the desert several years back. A gas station, a grocery, and a bar popped up just down the way where two roads intersected. A few other buildings and houses were built on that corner stretch of desert. People from all over came for gas or beer or groceries. The buses for school picked up and then dropped off children at the side of the gas station's parking lot. One of the roads turned north into rez land and on into Colorado. More and more traffic passed through, especially in the winter, as skiers and snowboarders used the rez as a shortcut for Durango and the other slopes in the Southern San Juan Mountains.

"I picked up Chicken Noodle this morning," people told his grandmother while she sold breakfast burritos from the back of her green Oldsmobile.

"I wish you wouldn't," she replied.

"He is growing tall."

"Two dollars," she said. She pointed her head, lips pressed together, to a blue Maxwell House coffee can on the roof of her car.

People came together around her car to talk. This summer there had been a lot of talk.

"They found him stretched to stakes."

"His stomach was open, split up the middle, flapped over on either side."

"A rancher found him."

"No, I heard it was Navajo police. Sheep had been missing."

"He was stretched long ways straight as an arrow."

"What direction was he pointing?"

"It was coyotes."

"Coyotes don't put his head on a pillow."

"It's not a pillow. It's a basket."

"That's right a basket with organs scooped out of his belly into the bowl of the basket."

"Did the others have baskets?"

At times, there was nothing to say about the secrets of the desert and the people stood around the car in silence mulling over questions already asked.

"How many is it now?"

"Ten."

"No, it's not ten yet. The next one will be ten."

Later, at home, people whispered, "It's a witch." Then, they went outside to sweep the leaves and dust from the front all the way to the door.

"Next," Chicken Noodle's grandmother said in the middle of all the whispers and side conversations. She listened as they spoke. She knew her own versions of the stories. She reached into her car for another burrito.

The burritos, wrapped in silver foil, made the Come and Go gas station a popular place during the week. A line of cars, tailpipes smoking, circled around the gas grocery and back into the flat lot behind it. This summer, the gloníís at night lined up opposite. They snaked from the lot to the bathroom on the side of the station. At least they did on Saturday night when Cindy was doing whatever it was she did in that bathroom. Cindy attended the Catholic school. She always wore her skirt with a white button up shirt, her uniform, complete with socks pulled up to her knees over stockings that she wore because she was always so cold. A lot of people, including her father, called her a whore. Her legs were pretty.

"It's no big deal," she told him on the way to school.

"So what are you doing?" he asked.

"None of your bee's wax," she said.

When they laughed, grandmother told them to be quiet.

His grandmother disapproved of Cindy and Chicken Noodle being friends. Grandmother told him to stay away from Cindy, although those two spent a whole lot of time together, so it was weird that she made such a big deal about it.

All summer long Chicken Noodle thought about Cindy when he stood at the gas station waiting for a ride into the desert.

Chicken Noodle sat outside the gas station's glass doors and waited.

Mr. John, last year's home room teacher, gave him a ride. He could do without the small talk, but even when he had to deal with Mr. John asking him about school, it was okay because it was like paying a price for the ride—a very reasonable price, unlike the price he paid for his disobedience when he next saw his grandmother. Her eyes darkened, and after doling out punishment, she stayed silent for days after this rebellion.

"How's school?"

Chicken Noodle nodded.

"You keeping up with," Mr. John paused, he always rearranged words in his head like editing a paper, "well how is school this year?"

Chicken Noodle nodded.

He never asked to be dropped off at the same place. It always depended. Today, he hiked along dried up creek beds, and followed the edge of a rock slide stepping around broken bottles. As he hiked, he held onto the shoulder straps of his backpack. It made him feel like a paratrooper waiting to pull a rip cord.

A coyote barked and the breeze turned cool. Evening was on its way. The low light filtered color out of the desert leaving a deep burnt sienna hue. His grandfather said afternoon light reminded him of the color of blood.

The silver-wrapped burrito nested on top of a folded burlap sack down at the bottom of his backpack. Some days he brought jerky. It mingled with the gloves and the knife and other small odds and ends—a wad of string, a piece of rope, and bent tent stakes.

The late sun lingered into the afternoon. Chicken Noodle scoured rockslide after rockslide walking deeper into the desert. The sun finally dropped below the mesa and a long shadow stretched out and wiggled in all directions filling the gaps and creases of the pocked desert. Darkness was not slow in coming. Night fell in a heavy way. It fell quickly, pulled as if connected to gravity, into place.

Then he saw it. The snake curved, leaving a rut in the sand as it twisted forward. He didn't move for a moment, marking where the snake was heading.

"Watch your footsteps," his grandfather would say. When he was little, it made him laugh. They felt even the slightest vibrations though, so he did just that.

"Snakes rest on the eardrum of the earth," his grandfather would say as he knelt to touch the warmth of the ground. He had a pull and connection to the desert, but the Western rattlesnake was like a brother, a favorite family member, to his grandfather.

Chicken Noodle lied earlier. He was catching a baby rattlesnake for his grandfather as a birthday present. It was a surprise his grandmother wouldn't be happy about. It was a symbol in the household, and it was rare to hear either of his grandparents talk about it. The story of the snake wrapped around the story of his mother. They intertwined, so over the years Chicken Noodle collected solitary bits of story like strands of left over yarn and he stitched the threads together, bit by bit, like trying to remember a fragmented and almost forgotten dream.

Chicken Noodle followed the snake through a tumble of rocks. Creeping along, he bent over and moved slowly across the rocks. He used his hands as much as his feet to keep his weight spread out. He was a spider scuttling over the terrain.

The snake paused just in front of Chicken Noodle. He leaned forward, grabbed, and missed. It slithered down a bank.

Chicken Noodle jumped to his feet and quickly tracked in the moonlight. The light silvered the rocks and the sand and the darting snake. It passed a buried boulder, just the top showing, like an iceberg floating in a desert sea. The snake's body flowed along the sandy places, undulating as it propelled forward.

It stopped.

Chicken Noodle slowed and crept up to the snake. He reached out his hand, his fingers stretched out like the forked tongue of a reptile feeling the air. Chicken Noodle steadied his hand and grabbed out at the snake for a second time.

He touched the cool body, but the snake slipped out of his grasp into the base of a half-buried desert rock.

He sat down on the cool clay soil. He had walked far into the desert, and he was going to be very late getting home and his grandmother was going to be very unhappy. He would probably be made to turn the garden over by himself, to put it to bed for the winter, if she had finished cutting and bundling today.

Before bodies showed up in the desert, Chicken Noodle spent whole weekends in the shivery night. His grandfather said shivering helped the people keep awake. They spent chunks of summer following dusty tracks deep into lonely places of desert. Some nights they walked all night until birds began their morning routines. Chicken Noodle stayed an arm's length behind his grandfather. Grandfather warned him of being in the desert alone at dark.

Yips and barks faded in and out with the cool night wind. Chicken Noodle heard wings in the air, but he couldn't see anything.

Then, as if being born into the desert, the snake moved its head out of the mini hollow at the base of the rock and began to push its body into the night.

Chicken Noodle sat very still. The snake was small, and the light faint. Catching it now was unwise. The thin light of the moon was tricky and since judging speed and distance was vital to catching a rattlesnake with only your hands he knew he should leave it alone.

He and his grandfather would track into the night but they always waited to catch anything until the light of early morning, but now might be his last chance. So, he shifted his weight.

A quick grab with thumb and forefinger just behind its arrow shaped head and although the rattlesnake twisted in his grasp he had it.

He turned at a scrape behind him pivoting on his toes, the snake swinging in his grip. A coyote sat on the bank he just scrambled down. The moon played tricks. The skin silver, like everything else in the moonlight, shifted, even while still. It shifted like it was still settling into place, almost like a snake might look shrugging back into its skin instead of shedding out of it. The coyote stood. It was a big animal. Tail still and stiff, like a rudder, it circled Chicken Noodle. The eyes startled him.

"Grandmother?"

The coyote stopped pacing at the sound of his voice. After a moment of staring, it stepped back and trotted into the darkness.

Chicken Noodle listened to the quieting steps until they muted, and then he listened to his heart beat until it quieted.

Then he sat down on the desert floor and cried.

After a time, the cold air settled around him and cooled him off, and now shivering in the cold Chicken Noodle wiped his face on his shirt sleeve. He uncurled the snake's body from his wrist and dropped the snake into the burlap sack. After winding the top shut with some string, he zipped up his backpack and stood.

Hitching home at night was a challenge. Once in a while, his orange touk grabbed the attention of someone driving back in from Albuquerque. Saturdays were Trader Joe days for a lot of people, and during the school year, Saturdays were desert days for Chicken Noodle. But like tonight, Chicken Noodle didn't always make it out to the road by a decent time.

Hitching was a numbers game. At night, the odds were worse than cards at a blackjack table. That's where the prickly pear came into the picture. The low lying desert cacti were abundant. He would cut off three ears with his knife and scrape away the tiny spines until he had three smooth flatbread shaped pieces of cactus. He pulled his orange gloves from the front pocket of his book bag and then pulled the gloves over two of the cactus ears and then waited for a car to pass.

"Here we go," he said to himself when car lights appeared.

It could take a while for the car to get to him, but he juggled anyway. The prickly pear leaves felt nice. They weighed just right when they landed in his hand and they hung in the air just right when he released them back into the night.

One bright orange glove, weighted with cactus, then the naked one, and then the next orange one. He would catch, flip, catch, flip, catch, and flip until the car either stopped or passed him.

"A bit late to be juggling," drivers said.

Chicken Noodle nodded.

"Where you headed?"

"Not far."

Chicken Noodle made it to the road when brake lights stared back at him. A big station wagon pulled to the side. The red lights blinked a couple times as the car pulled over and then they just stared. They were a pair of red eyes watching him walk up to the wagon. The station wagon looked familiar.

He wondered how it knew to stop, how the driver saw him. He hadn't even looked for a prickly pear, much less started juggling. A ride's a ride though.

Looking into the passenger window, Chicken Noodle saw him. The man in the sunglasses stared back through the framed arch of the car window. In all of his dreams the man in the sunglasses stood at a gate where time and place differed depending on which side of the gate you focused. The window opening was like that gate. The inside of the car seemed darker and colder than the outside. The side of the man's thin face reflected in the dark glass of the driver's side window. The image and the sunglasses and the smell of the car directly linked to his dreams, but, like in a dream, Chicken Noodle's body did things without consultation with his mind. The man's silver bracelets with embedded turquoise and beads looped into chains around his neck. Chicken Noodle looked down at his own big belt buckle and his jeans and his boots, and he thought of something his grandfather always said. It was something that never occurred to him before in his dreams.

"Cowboys wanna be Indians and Indians wanna be cowboys," he said.

"What's that?" asked the driver.

"Nothing."

"Where you headed?" The man said air instead of where.

"Down the way a bit."

"Well," the man grinned, "get in."

"Right," Chicken Noodle said quietly, but he took a small step back.

It surprised him that he reached for the handle anyway and how easily the car door opened. He placed his book bag into the front floor board. Why was he getting in? He squirmed as he pulled the door closed. Something in the seat kept him from settling. He lifted his leg and pulled a big roll of duct tape from under it.

"Toss that back," the man grinned.

Chicken Noodle fidgeted. He pulled the seat belt across his body. There were always more cars. What was he doing in this car? His lack of control was, as always, frustrating. He shivered—zero to the bone. The car smelled like hospital gloves or maybe belly buttons. The vents exhaled a cold steady flow of air.

The man looked over at him. Chicken Noodle couldn't see the man's eyes through the black sunglasses, but he saw his own face.

He saw twin images of his own face.

They pulled off the shoulder and started driving down the road. "I've been watching you," the man said, "You've pretty lips."

Chicken Noodle nodded.

"Anyone ever tell you that before?"

Chicken Noodle shook his head. He toed his bag.

The man reached over and brushed the back of his white fingers along his knee. Chicken Noodle didn't like it. He thought of Cindy, standing in the light of the gas station parking lot. He thought of grandmother selling burritos. He thought of that motel room that he could never enter.

"Maybe we should pull over for a bit," said the man. The man grabbed himself with his white fingers and made a noise. It sounded like air leaking through a cracked window, and Chicken Noodle didn't like it.

"That's okay," said Chicken Noodle.

The man grabbed his knee, cupped it as if it were a gear shift.

"Here is fine," said Chicken Noodle. His right hand found the door latch.

"No," said the man.

Ahead of them, Chicken Noodle thought he saw a dog step onto the road into the weak headlights of the station wagon. The man in the sunglasses saw it too and slowed down. It was a coyote. It stood still in the middle of the pavement.

The man in the sunglasses braked. He put both hands back on the steering wheel and the station wagon jerked to a stop right in front of the animal. The coyote stood its ground in the dim headlights. Chicken Noodle opened the passenger door. The dome light of the car turned on when the door opened and the light was harsh and yellow. Chicken Noodle squinted at it and for a moment it was mesmerizing, a hypnotist's charm swinging from a cord.

His left hand pushed down the seatbelt clasp, but the man grabbed and held onto his hand so hard he couldn't depress it. With the door open, Chicken Noodle reached down and unzipped his book bag. He pulled the burlap sack to his lap and uncoiled the cinched string.

The snake lifted its head from the opening, tongue tasting air.

Chicken Noodle grabbed behind the jaw, firm but gentle and the body of the snake arched and wrapped around his wrist.

The man let go of Chicken Noodle's hand when he saw the snake.

"Fuck," he leaned away from Chicken Noodle, pressing his body into the driver's side door.

The seatbelt popped loose.

The rattlesnake clicked its one bead at the tip of its tail faintly, again and again, like a stone in the groove of a tire.

"Get out," the man hissed.

The man in the sunglasses pushed at Chicken Noodle's shoulder, and Chicken Noodle scrambled backwards and fell out the car door with the snake around his wrist.

The station wagon revved forward and Chicken Noodle closed his eyes, and breathed, and listened to the engine quiet as the man in the sunglasses put distance between them.

Holding the snake, he sat up off the rough cold pavement.

The sky shone lighter than he remembered. The sun highlighted the peaks of the mountains. Had he been out all night? He thought about his mother. He couldn't really remember her. His grandfather found her unconscious with a snake bite. He put her in the truck and raced to town. Nobody ever finished that story, but he knew how it ended of course.

The rattlesnake adjusted its thin body around Chicken Noodle's wrist. He cradled the snake with both hands making sure to keep his fingers firm on the head, and then he thought about his grandmother. Would she say this was a dream too? Maybe he would wake up in a moment to bright sunshine exorcising the characters and landscapes that were all woven together in the fabric of his mind.

Far off yips called back and forth.

Chicken Noodle thought about what grandmother said after they discovered a fox in the coop.

"The desert's beauty is without meaning if not balanced with hardship." She said it as they repaired the hole in the chicken coop where the fox played out his mischief.

"Balanced with hardship?" He rolled his eyes and said, "Grand-mother."

Later, after mending and weaving the bent wires, she pointed to a set of tracks leading away from the coop. "The thread of a story can be followed from any point along its spool," Grandmother said. She smiled at him, patted him on the shoulder, and went back to the garden.

The morning star, a silver speck, shone steady in the dim light of the eastern sky above the dark road where the thin man in the black sunglasses vanished.

Chicken Noodle walked the winding road. In the early light, it is a gray snake, mother of all snakes, granting him a ride on her wide back. Wind plays a game with the ditch weeds, and the early morning voices of the desert come and go with the wind. A garrulous finch lands on a fence wire. It chirps and chirps under the morning sky.

The sun warms his head. He is without his things. The man in the sunglasses is somewhere down the road heading toward town with his touk and backpack in the front seat. The snake, body wrapped around his wrist and clinging like duct tape, points in the direction of town. Its tongue flicks the air.

Transmigration

After my parents performed my burial, I stayed perched as a goldfinch in the branches of the tiny desert willow. Mountain snows swept the landscape before long sunshine and hard rain turned back into the days of lingering cold and flying snow, and all the while I stayed perched in the willow.

As they wandered across the evening horizon, I saw the outline of foxes and wolves and lone coyotes prowling their daily errands. They leaned into the wind with their heads down in the cold, and when the days warmed, they lingered more often, sometimes sitting in the embrace of summer wind. They were my only company.

One spring morning, an old woman with swirling skirts, and hair so dark it had the stars caught in it, stopped to touch the spines of a prickly pear. She pulled one of the purple blooms of my willow tree to her nose.

"Dear Goldfinch," she said, "You have lost your way." The words appeared directly in my mind. She didn't care to break the stillness of the afternoon.

I shuffled my feathers and squeezed my talons into the soft bark of the willow.

"You are no longer where you think you are," she said. "You are no longer in the fifth world. Come, follow me."

The fifth world was created in the beginning for all the clans, and it is where the people, the clans, still live today, in the beauty of the southwest, at the foot of the great mountain range.

I hopped up the branch, away. I chirped loud crisp calls. But there was no one to help me. I lost my family, my body, my voice.

Changing Woman lifted her arms, continued to speak without words. Feelings and colors, more vibrant than I had ever imagined, filtered up through the branches and settled along the edges of my olive feathers. The bright quicksilver that edged my feathers now shimmered, her power. I shook my feathers fat around my body, but I glowed brighter and brighter. The glow bled out of the edges and covered every feather.

"My dear, now I can see you. No matter where you are, I am with you, watching and guiding."

Up another branch, and another until the crown of the willow was my only protection, I hopped.

"Kaila," she said. "I know you. You are one of my many daughters."

I spread my wings and flew from the willow, and it was not by choice. As if Changing Woman controlled my reflexes, I flew. Down from the branches of the willow I landed in the cup of her hand. As if filled with water, her hand shimmered and the power of the wind and the sun ebbed inside of it. She took a step to the turtle-backed boulder. To my surprise, we walked right past it. My imprisonment vanished.

"Don't be surprised, little one," she said, "You have been free to fly for quite some time."

We strolled along the horizon for what may have been days or hours. Time played no role in our travel, and the sun sat in its descent and cast its light before us. We arrived at a ragged coast. The rocky shore broke the travelling waves. Each wave carried a story from far off shores and tumbled them out at our feet. There the sun continued.

With a flap of my wings I followed my mother through the front door of my childhood home. I darted into the front room just before she shut the door, before she shut in the darkness. It was dark and the air in the house felt heavy. It was the tense air of an unresolved quarrel. I remembered the placement of everything. There were tiny herbs by the window and shoes kicked off under the kitchen table. A tea tin with the poison my mother fed my father sat on the counter.

When Changing Woman showed stories, there was no past or

future, all memories lay out before me, swirling, non-linear. Time was a great lake, stilled by solitude. It was not a flowing river. Changing Woman's stories arrived from everywhere at once. In the word pictures that hovered in the air of Changing Woman's hogan, I saw my mother wrap the green thread tea with herbs to keep my father sick. I watched my mother push everyone away. I watched my mother cripple with regret.

Father coughed, hidden in his room.

Mother passed his room to the door of Chicken Noodle's room.

The door opened and the darkness lifted. The moon was bright in the window. My son slept with his face turned to the door. He was a man now, my Noodle. It was difficult to look away from his face.

The last time I had seen him he was a wobble-kneed toddler. Seeing Chicken Noodle again was as unbelievable as turning into a songbird, but knowing the one is possible doesn't make believing in the other easy. He had grown into a version of his father, another face faded from my memory. I lost Chicken Noodle's father first, while still pregnant, to a shooting downtown. I still hold those tears back.

I flew into the room before Mother closed the door.

"Grandson," she said. The low whisper of her voice murmured.

From the bottom of her bag, she lifted the severed head of a rattlesnake into the dark. She turned the snakehead. The black eyes were empty pits in the darkness of the bedroom. Her hand trembled. She raised the head to her face. The dead eyes of the one locked with the eyes of the other. She shifted her weight as if in a dance and stepped to the bed. With the snake, in her palm, she stared down at my sleeping boy.

"Mother," I said. The word a chirp as a sense of futility settled the room. The chirp went unheard.

"Grandson," she said again. She spoke louder into the room, but Noodle continued to sleep.

Her cheeks were streaked. I noticed, at some point, she had covered herself in ash.

"Mother," I repeated. "Mother."

She could not hear me. I flapped my wings. I tried to land on her

139

shoulders, but everything in the room, including my mother, ignored my physical presence.

She had heard my chirps. For a moment, she had even heard my words of warning. Unable to influence her anymore, I flew around the room. I hovered and flapped rapid beats with my wings. My head banged against the hard surface of the ceiling. The stucco texture pulled feathers from my crown and my feathers ruffled to a mess. A frenzy rose inside of me. I could not interact with anything but the walls.

The room was a cage, and my light body struggled to move. Every wing beat felt like the last. Hovering used too much energy and I dropped to the covers of the bed. The shock of landing on the bed was replaced by the shock of the bright quicksilver glow edged along my feathers. My feathers vibrated and pulled, and I picked at a spot of molting feathers with my beak.

Mother sat on the side of the bed. If she saw a little bird scratching molt from its wings, she didn't react. I puffed up round trying to shake the glow from my feathers, trying to break out of this body.

After molding the clans from her own skin, Changing Woman built a hogan in the west, in another world, in another afterlife. She moved there long ago. The water crashed into itself along the rocks, and for many days the waves entertained us with their chatter. In time, I learned the stories of the old woman as well.

Many nights, I listened and watched stories take life. Words carried the blues, reds, and greens, the patterns of story. Images burst. Yellow trails bounced from the walls and dripped down the air like wet paint. As if the air between us was made of hundreds of clear sheets, the dripping colors formed in layers and there the stories took shape before me. The stories of my life and those I loved replayed often—my father's struggle with Vietnam, my mother's struggle with the parts of my father Vietnam left her.

The stories I learned about Changing Woman as a child were different than the stories I watched unfold here. As if this place had its own balance, as if it was its own garden in need of tending. There were others, many song birds and warblers, located in a constant stream of migration. They collected in the canopies of the forests along the coast around her hogan, and spoke of how she must be Changing Woman. They spoke of how she had lived in solitude for so long, since the days when life had been given to the people. A flock of songbirds followed us throughout the day. The whisk of leaves and feathers and the chorus, the chatter and song of her many bird companions stayed the movement of the forest.

During an afternoon walk the songbird's frenzy overhead escalated. Warning calls warbled back and forth in the canopies, buzzed and agitated.

"I hear the cry of your flock," said a voice. "I know you are near."

After warning her of the prying eyes, the flock led her deeper into the forest along hidden paths guiding her through shortcuts amidst the jubilee of bird song. Trickster roamed her world. Changing Woman avoided him.

"I hear your flock scatter. They flee as if I threatened danger," said Trickster.

"Come, little bird. This way," said Changing Woman. The canopies overhead fluttered like a wind blowing through an open window.

Hundreds of song birds perched and flew and perched, directing our new path in a loop of movement. Tail flicks flashed yellow and red feathers.

"Finch, who do you think placed the stars in the sky?" said Trickster. "How could I mean you harm?"

I flew from left shoulder to right shoulder, gripping Changing Woman's shirt with the curl of my claws.

"Be still, little one," she said.

"I will find your finch," said Trickster.

The forest shifted and his voice quit. Chirping birdsong settled around us. The sharp warnings gave way to trill of melody. Like stepping through the curtain, from one room to another, we stepped into the clearing of the hogan, led through space by the magic of Changing Woman's birds.

That evening, the hogan darkened, the way it did before the telling of a story, a storm cloud shading an afternoon. Color spread like the beginning of rain drops splashing into the space of the room, pooling from the memories of the past. The flows of memory were currents swirling outside the well of time.

Drops slapped waxy leaves. The drumming of heavy rain moved down the mountainside. A ditch ran along the edge of a worn trail. Water streamed down the trail and filled the ditch. At an embankment, where the trail turned uphill, a fox stepped, for a moment, into the open. The fox slipped back under a broad leaf. It was my mother.

Changing Woman showed many stories of my mother following my father through the jungles of Vietnam, following in her fox form.

When I asked Changing Woman why she was there, she said there was always a reason beside the one that seemed clear.

Four soldiers crouched in the undergrowth, on the other side of the trail. Behind the group two Viet Cong men, dressed in khakis, in the color of mud, crept. The soldiers watched rain puddle the trail before them, unaware of the two Viet Cong creeping behind them. The occasional leaf moved in the undergrowth. Thick jungle canopy shed water like a tarp and the wet poured down. The two Viet Cong pulled themselves along with their elbows. They smashed ruts into the jungle floor as they crawled. Their bodies flattened the grasses like the passing slither of great snakes. Vigilant, the men's eyes were large. Rainfall increased and every leaf bobbed. The drumming of the rain blocked every other sound.

"What do you think, Chief?" asked one of the men. Water dripped from his nose.

"Hard to tell," was the reply. "Been raining too long."

Just behind the embankment, where the four men crawled up earlier, the boys stopped their crawl. Pressed against the mud the two Viet Cong could have been discarded bodies forgotten after a fight. But they were not discarded and they worked together without speaking. Each worked off the other in the comfortable knowing of habit. This was not the first ambush, the first trip line the two set.

They unspooled wire between them and staked bamboo into the ground, wrapping the wire in place around each stake then stringing it across to the other. One of them pulled a grenade from his pocket and attached its pin to the tripwire.

I saw the fox, my mother, circle the entire group.

"Let's push back and move up the trail," said the first man again, "lead us out, Chief."

My father slid down the muck. The two boys crept away. They raked the ground with their fingers trying to raise the flattened trail they were leaving behind. In the rain, it didn't matter. Everything pooled and dripped and one mud pit looked like another.

My father stood. He checked over his shoulder, and then he stepped forward. The trip wire, dulled by mud, strung under a lean of grasses.

He took another step toward the wire. The rain fell hard. He wiped his eyes with the back of his hand. The bobbing jungle leaves opened gaps in the darkness, and everything moved. He motioned for the others to follow. His careful step landed next to the wire. Mud sucked up with it. His next step would yank the pin from the grenade.

I squirmed when the boot lifted. My feathers puffed big around my body. I hopped on my perch. The screen of color in the hogan seeped into my mind and pushed everything to the fringe so the memory felt real, almost as if it were happening and not the memory of something from the past.

My mother darted into view and paused long enough for my father to see her. She raised a wet paw, shook water free from her purple coat, and stepped back into the undergrowth. He raised his hand above his shoulder and curled his fingers into a fist. Rain splashed across the knuckles. He stepped backwards and placed his boot back into the same muddy print where it had just been.

"There's the fox," he said.

"The Indian won't give it a rest," said the tall skinny one.

"Quiet."

My father kneeled down. He reached out and ran a finger along the wire. The wire faded and the sound of the heavy rain lifted as if it moved down the valley. The edges of the hogan flickered and the memory scene blurred.

"There you are," Trickster said. His voice jarred, rocks sliding in a pile. He stood in the doorway of the hogan.

Trickster visited once before. I stayed quiet in the trees, my olive feathers blending in amongst the leaves. He looked plain, but his face twisted in the light. I hopped to a higher branch. The yellow eyes of the trickster never blinked. The fabric of Changing Woman's swirling skirts shifted and moved, in constant motion, like the heat of an afternoon rising from a sunbaked rock, and the Trickster was like the baked rock, ever slow to change.

Today, Trickster walked through the hogan door, interrupting Changing Woman's stories. I was too slow, slowed from the vision of my father fighting the muck of Vietnam.

"Well," he said, "there you are. The little birdie who doesn't want to be found."

"There has been talk of this little addition to your flock," he said. Trickster's yellow eyes stayed on me, but he was now talking to Changing Woman.

"She will push ripples along, like a branch stuck in a river, but then you know that, don't you?" Trickster pointed his finger into the air and turned to Changing Woman.

Changing Woman stood. She flattened her dress down her stomach. Her hair lifted and floated and hung straight down her back all at the same time. She was still but in motion, and often she spoke without moving her mouth. The words reached out and teased themselves into my thoughts.

"She is here now," said Changing Woman, "and she is my guest. I am coaxing her voice back into the world."

"Her wings need to be clipped," said Trickster, "she must stay in the west. The body she has now suits her."

"Where would she go?"

"She is not as balanced as you think. She yearns for her people. "

"We all do."

"Not I. Come with me, little bird." Trickster reached for me. I leaned away. The same tug I felt when Changing Woman found me pulled me from my perch. I flexed my claws.

"She is not yours," said Changing Woman.

His eyes flashed the color of blood. He reached higher. I hopped back.

"Let's see if we can't keep you in that body," said Trickster.

"Old man, you always make mistakes, and they are with trouble in mind."

"I only want to help our little birdie."

"It is time you leave my hogan, old man," said Changing Woman. With a twirl, she turned the hogan around. Trickster spun out of the opening of the door and disappeared into the dark. The front door faced east instead of west, and where once a yellow sun peaked now the shine of the moon spilled white into the room. Changing Woman reached and cupped my frail body in her hand. I floated in her shimmer, in that lake of possibility. She carried me through the door, and in that moment she gave me new life.

Before my time in the afterlife, before Changing Woman, before Trickster, before I flew behind my body as a goldfinch, I remember the ceremony of my life fading, my life ending. Did I know I would be able to follow my death experience, a little bird perched in the shrub of a shade tree watching the pass of afternoon?

After the rattlesnake bite, my mother soothed my arm. She placed me on the couch and splinted my arm still and cooled my forehead with a wet cloth. The sweet smell of crushed herbs hovered over me. We were miles from anywhere and had to wait for my father to return with the truck.

"Stay with me, daughter," she said.

"I will," I said. "Don't worry, I will."

She calmed the house and everything in it. Even Chicken Noodle stilled, playing in a corner. My body stilled as well. My blood thumped through my veins slowly, long pauses between each heartbeat kept the poison from spilling right away into my body. Spill it did though. After the hours of the afternoon turned to evening, I saw my mother's jaws clench and her eyes turn dark.

Chicken Noodle stood at the couch and on wobble legs reached out a hand to touch the splint keeping my arm straight. He smiled at me. The poison driving to my heart could not hinder the power of that heartbreak. He smiled and then plopped down on the rug and crawled off to explore another corner. That small grin from my son sat with me for a moment, it wrapped its arms around me, and then the sound of my father's tires churned gravel onto the undercarriage of his truck. My mother stopped running her fingers along the skin around the poultice.

The screen door banged the side of the house.

"You never let them go!" Mother screamed.

"What have you done?"

"What have you done?" she screamed. She turned back in from the outside. I saw her dark silhouette outlined from the screen door.

Afternoon light pushed through the wire of the screen door and faded at the doorway, deterred by darkness.

My father stepped through the door, and his outline melded into the shape of my mother, and the two stood there like a great, many-limbed beast. They whispered in the house, but I could hear them, I could feel them, like the textures of so many fabrics. I could feel their words, and it was the first moment my body began to slip away from me.

"Your grandson was pushing the lids all morning," my mother said. "How many times has she asked for you to get rid of them?" One of the arms of the great beast in the living room pointed in my direction.

"How long has it been?" My father asked. "Where were you?"

"Where were you?" Mother's voice shook and a tremor ran through the air. A shiver turned my skin cold, and I slipped even further away, pushed from the space of the room. "Always out looking for those snakes."

My father leaned down and turned my palm into the light.

"Kaila," he said. My name settled over my body like the light billow of a bed cloth. I loved him for it. I loved him for the gentle way he said my name, and at that moment I forgave my father for all the closed doors that hid my weeping from him and all the open doors that let him stumble into the arms of his demons.

The screen door was still open. Faint yips and barks of desert coyotes floated into the house. The smell of rain followed.

My father stood. His outline melded into my mother's again.

"The thing is," said the great monster at my side.

The sound of rain hit harder.

Then the amalgam in the dark said it, and it may not have said it very loudly, but to me words travelled without sound anyway, "We got to figure out how to forgive ourselves." I heard it, a rough woolen bed spread prickling my skin.

I forgive you. I couldn't speak it. I could only think it.

And then they were carrying me to the pickup. They tied me down in the rain, in the bed of the truck. With the rest of my family in the cab the tires skidded over gravel.

But it was too late. I believe we all knew it. I wasn't able to hold onto anything anymore, like dropping a cup to the floor, having it slip through your fingers. But instead of a cup, it was my desire to be with my family. Instead of my fingers, it was my grasp on everything I knew. In the end, it didn't matter how much I tried to hold on to that cup. I still dropped it.

There was a point where I wasn't connected anymore. I was tethered above my father's Ford Ranger, a bird chained in the wind dragged in the same direction looking down on a body no longer mine. After the hospital, we drove back home. They still had me tied down, but I was wrapped in a hospital sheet, covered in gauzy white, the silk of a widow, and I was pulled through the air still attached but no longer belonging.

That night my parents placed Chicken Noodle in his bed, and after securing my body on a wooden stretcher, they walked in silence toward the mountains. All night they walked. I hovered close sometimes, a tiny finch in the wind, I zoomed back and forth over the terrain as my parents dragged my body into the desert and my body dragged me into the afterlife.

We stopped moving at a small flat by the hunched shell of a great turtle, turned old and worn, a boulder long forgotten in the desert.

They spread ash on their skin. They placed my body on the back side of another boulder, in a cot-like crevice. They did not speak. A small fire fed on the dried thorns my father used to broom their tracks. It burned the wooden stretchers, too. The gray smoke whipped around my parents. It must have stung their eyes. Their tears streaked the ash covering their faces. They left the flat, and although I wanted to follow, although I wanted to be chained to their movement, I was imprisoned as if a room with invisible walls had been placed around my body. I could fly as far as the top of a stunted tree growing next to my body. From the branches of the willow, their backs disappeared down the slope and as they faded from sight, my life faded from the expanse of a great world to the slight twigs of a willow tree.

For many years then, how many I don't know, I perched there, alone, and watched the winter turn to summer and the summer return to winter. Every spring, the willow bloomed purple trumpets. The flash of hummingbirds invaded my branches. When the blooms faded, I was alone again through the heat of summer and the cold of winter. After Changing Woman found me and took me west, I don't remember flowers aging, I don't remember winters losing their grip to spring or summer turning to winter. In the West, time was not a river. Time was a high mountain lake, pooled still, protected by cliffs and walls.

That moment in the hogan when Changing Woman snatched me from Trickster, my wings began to drag me down to earth. Before he could chain me down, keeping me from entering the fifth world again, she picked me up and walked through that eastern facing door of her hogan. On the other side, old and brittle, she leaned on a cane as if the doorway had doubled her age. Before us the little desert willow tree waited and she sat me in it.

"There, little Goldfinch, you are needed here. I will miss your afternoon song," she said. She turned to her hogan. "I have always known this moment. Trickster underestimates the power of a moment." She closed the door and was gone.

Sadness settled around me when she closed that door. It felt like morning dew beading on my feathers. If felt like the sun disappearing behind a mountain's ridge. Did Changing Woman prepare me for something? Did she just bring me back to this clearing, this cage, to endure an eternity of solitude?

"You have been free to fly for quite some time," she said when she first found me.

I realized a presence nearby and lifted my head. Still perched in the willow as if I had never been absent I turned my head down to see my mother, a much older, and more worn version of my mother.

Her black hair now streaked with white and her body sunken into itself. The fabric of her clothing spoke with the faded colors of a wearied life. In her hands stretched the body of a rattlesnake. Her hands pulled the snake's body tight in front of her. My mother's grip strangled the snake just behind its bony head.

"You should have prepared two graves, snake," my mother said. "When you sank your poison into my family, you should have feared leaving me untouched."

My mother swung the body by the tail. It whipped across the boulder's back.

She bent the neck towards her mouth and cracked its spine in half with her teeth. The crack ended all sound for a moment. Even the wind stayed its movement. She dropped the separated snake into the dirt.

The cool air stilled. A slippery feeling I had not felt in many years reminded me, urged me, to speak. My body tingled with the weight of this world. My feathers were heavy on my shoulders, and I grasped harder my perch.

My mother kneeled with her forehead on the ground.

Coyotes yipped.

The sun had long followed its path behind the mountains and the brightness of the moon began its rise. My mother trembled in the quiet. I chirped, more warning than song.

"Mother," I said.

She turned her head to look past each shoulder.

"Daughter," she said, "Kaila."

She took out the kitchen knife from her old weaved bag. It was the bag she carried into the desert when we gathered the pinion nuts and the sage. My mother turned the point towards her and with her other hand she felt her stomach.

I chirped again. Another warning, and she turned her head a bit as she searched the branches of the willow.

"Mother, this is a mistake," I said.

"No, my Daughter."

The wind settled in front of the leftover heat of the day. The rocks and cliffs radiated into the cool nighttime air. The warm air moved and dropped cold down the slopes and ruffled the feathers on my back.

"I have been to the end of the earth, I have been to the end of the waters, I have been to the end of the sky, and now I am here at the end of the mountains—"

"Mother," I called out for a third time, and this time I spoke without birdsong. I perched next to her. I was close enough to hold her hand yet she could not see me.

She picked up the severed head of the rattle snake. "Yes, Daughter, yes," she rubbed the head. She rubbed between the eyes with her thumb, "Yes, you are right. It is a mistake."

I stayed quiet, afraid of what currents my interruption would bring.

"Your father chose long ago, did he not?" She turned the decapitated head in her hand. "He chose his own family. He chose over you and me. That was the mistake. He is the one who has lived too long. It is not me."

"Kaila, forgive me," my mother stood and repeated her words, "Forgive me."

I flew after her. The wind felt like a billowy sheet. She picked her way down the path. In the way a shrieking wind could tear across a valley, she vanished, crossing time and place in a single step. Changing Woman showed me the owl talisman and the creeping fox that was my mother keeping watch over my father's patrol during the war. I breathed in when my mother took flight and flew from the kitchen window into the world. The power in that transformation opened my mind to what my mother could do. I circled in the air and searched for her footsteps, but they had been swept away.

Thanking Moon for his generous light, I flew just above the desert floor. From shrub to shrub down the mountain foot. The deep reds and stretched tans of the desert lay whitewashed before me. And then I heard the sobbing of my mother, and I saw the lights of our tiny home on the mesa. She stopped at the edge of the lot covered in the darkness of the desert.

"No, no, no," I heard her say, "It is too much."

"Wait, mother." She could not hear me. I chirped into the darkness. "Mother, you chose too." I said. Still she could not hear me.

Mother grabbed her hair, and fell to her knees again. This time she rocked back and forth until she leaned forward so her forehead touched cool earth.

"Kaila. Forgive me."

"Oh mother, what are you going to do?" I hovered above her head and then dropped down into the bushes next to her. Changing Woman had not shown me tonight's memory. But the many memory visions I watched in her hogan did prepare me for this moment.

After living through the eyes of my father as he slipped through the shadows of jungle or seeing the dream-walk of my mother take flight after him and guide him around obstacles, I understood the possibility of endless opportunity. I understood this chance to change outcome. It was a ripple forward in the cup of Changing Woman's hands.

After the light quit from the windows of the house, and after the moon moved across the sky, she rose to her feet.

In the dark my mother stood at the bed. She turned the snakehead in her hand, pinching the jaws and prying them open until the flat landscape of the mouth was interrupted only by the sharp barbs of fangs.

"Forgive me," my mother said. She pressed the sharp barbs of venom into his neck.

"Mother!" I screamed. Still no reaction.

Changing Woman's words floated into the room. Maybe I heard them. Maybe I remember then. "You have been free to fly for quite some time," she had said. Those words carried the weight of so much possibility, so much hope.

I began to shift. The bed sank under my weight. Feathers turned and dropped around me, some pulled together into long hair and my tiny body stretched and unbent out of shape, my arms and legs grew. The bones in my body grew heavy, dense, and the weight of the room, my life, gravity pushed down on my shoulders and my neck and my breasts. Just breathing in this human form was unfamiliar and difficult, moving almost painful.

Chicken Noodle twitched. He opened his eyes and grabbed my mother's wrist. He saw me sitting behind her. His eyes widened and he reached out in my direction.

The snakehead fell into the covers. Chicken Noodle put a hand on his neck. Then he reached for me, but instead touched my mother's cheek.

"Grandmother," he said, "why are you crying?"

"Mother, what are you doing?"

Turning her head our eyes met. "Kaila. You should not be here."

"Yet here I am. What are you doing?"

"You should not be here."

"Of all people, mother." I stood up, and she gasped.

"You are glowing." My arms smooth and soft under my hands still shimmered from the quicksilver-words of Changing Woman, from her power.

"Mother, I met her."

Mother fidgeted with the bag in her lap and stood. Chicken

Noodle sat up a little bit. He squinted in the early light. Beads of sweat collected along his forehead.

"You're naked," he said to me.

A knock on the bedroom door. The knob turned and my father's tired face moved in from the darkness of the house.

"Kaila." He said my name so that it barely passed his lips. It just hung and fell without enough air under it to keep it afloat. It was matter of fact and accepting.

"George," Mother said, "go back to bed."

He turned, more broken than I realized.

"She's poisoned him," I said. I stepped to the bed and reached into the covers and pulled the snake head into the light.

Chicken Noodle shivered.

"What have you done?" He said. He looked at mother and no one spoke.

She tapped him on the chest. "What I should have done years ago. Hurt you."

"Put on some clothes," he said to me. He didn't question how it was possible. He knew what he knew, and for my father that was good enough now. He leaned over the bed and grunted with the effort of lifting Chicken Noodle in his arms. "Meet me at the truck." He marched out of the room. Long heel first strides boomed through the quiet of the house.

"Mother, come with us."

Squinting her eyes, my mother shook her head. "You shouldn't be here," she said.

"You brought me here," I said.

The floor by the bed was a landscape of clothes, and I picked out a pair of jeans and a worn t-shirt with the face of a wolf peering out from it.

"I needed you," said my mother.

"I'm sorry," I said.

The repetition of the truck ride to town stilled our tongues. Instead of evening when he rushed to save me, it was morning, and at every turn the sky brightened. My father sat straight in his seat. I sat next to him with Chicken Noodle's clammy forehead in my lap.

His black hair stuck out in clumps. The last time I held my boy, I could hold him up with one arm, and now this man took up the cab and toxins formed runs of sweat on his skin. The weight of his body pushed against me through the curves. His long legs angled off the seat to the passenger side floorboards. My father gripped the steering wheel and held the corners hard. A never ending fence paralleled the road. A group of finches paced alongside the pickup. They landed on the fence and flew forward, landed and flew forward, a mesmerizing loop of movement.

"Those finches always made your mother think of you," my father said.

I may never know if she really was Changing Woman, but now in the cab of my father's truck, after waking up for the first time in thirteen years, after feeling the cool of the earth settle around my shoulders in the dawn hours, and after opening my eyes to the deserts of the four corners, I believe she may have been that old woman. I returned to my family for the first time in years. Changing Woman showed me second chances to thwart malicious ways. There was possibility thick in the air when she spoke of my yearning, my displacement, and although she believed my balance was achieved, the stories she wove traveled the steep slopes of forgiveness.

The sun showed itself, just a sliver, but the blood of desert rock flowed bright around us, and the finches looped along the fence line in search of desert thistle. Flashes of yellow guided us along the dirt road. Their song pulled the horizon forward, like a loose string pulled tight when mother bunched her herb bundles together at the kitchen table.

The gravel road came to an end. It was an empty morning in the desert. No car in any direction and my father pulled the pickup onto the road and roared toward town. The buildings were far closer than they should have been, and the finches kept pace, kept pushing us through the morning fabric of time.

ACKNOWLEDGMENTS

Some of these chapters first appeared in the following literary journals, sometimes in a different form:

"The Tale of Cindy Jack's Mother," *The Hungry Chimera*. Vol. 3. 2017

"Straight Piping," *The Fat Damsel*. Vol. 11. 2017

"The Gulf Stream," *The Best of Crab Fat Magazine 2016-2017*. 2017

"How the Butcher Bird Finds her Voice," *New Mexico Review*. May. 2017.

"If You Chase Two Rabbits," *Jelly Bucket*. Vol. 8. 2017

"For These are Wells Without Water," *The Windward Review*. Vol 15. 2017.

"The Secret of Old Man Gloom," *The Wild Word*. 2017.

"The Gulf Stream," *Crab Fat Magazine*. 2017.

"Trash," *The Dead Mule School of Southern Literature*. 2016.

In addition, "Cindy Jack and the Town Drunks" was a semi-finalist for the 2017 Tillie Olson Short Story Award, 2017, and "The Gulf Stream" was chosen for inclusion in *The Best of Crab Fat Magazine* Print Anthology 2016-2017.

The chapter "How the Butcher Bird Finds Her Voice " is dedicated to Sheldon Curley.

I am fortunate for the unconditional support I receive from my friends, family, and mentors. My mom and dad always supported my reading and writing, even though they often made me turn my flashlight off when I read under the covers after bedtime. Stefanie, Heinz, Kurt, Inge, and Christian: *Ihr seid alle irgendwie in diesem Buch.* My friends prompted many drafts and conversations about original content. Tine, Neil, Alex, Quint, Diz, Josh, Bryan, Martin, and Lisa read and responded or prodded at just the right times too. Julie, Bob, Derek, Young, and Jim, thank you for your patience in answering all of my questions all of the time. Especially Julie. You were right to push me. You still guide me around pitfalls.

Lynn. By taking a chance on me, you are fulfilling some long-held dreams, but your creativity and attention to detail need to be recognized here, as Five Oaks Press turns over another leaf.

Sheldon Curley I met in the nick of time because he set me straight on some crucial elements of this novel. It's a small world sometimes. Thank you for helping me spell.

Finally, my dearest. Mary Clai. You are the reader of every word, of every draft. You even read ideas or stories that don't make it past the trashcan. All the birds are for you.